D1196233

90 MILLION REASONS

Catherine Harte

print ISBN: 978-1-66784-649-1

ebook ISBN: 978-1-66784-650-7

Contents

Forward

"I just want to live to be 90 years old. I will have a party with a big cake. There will be balloons with the number 90 on them." Maisie, my grandmother, said this to me one day while we were having tea. She said it so confidently. She was 88 years old, and I was 17. I wondered why that was "enough" for her. Why didn't she want to live to be 100 years old?

She missed her husband, my grandfather Malachy. He passed away in 1963 on a cold November Sunday. It was after church. It had been 32 years since he had passed. 32 years was longer than the time she and Mal had been together. Maisie was a religious woman, and even in later years becoming a Eucharistic Minister. She was not afraid of dying. Heaven was a wonderful place where she would be reunited with those that had passed. She often played Irish songs, especially on Sunday. Fordham University in New York had a program "Ceol na nGael" which translated to The Music of the Irish. I didn't appreciate the music until I was much older. It also brings back so many memories of the days I had with my grandmother. Maisie is the reason I am who I am today. She introduced me to Ireland, not just the country, but the experience. I went to Ireland at the age of 14 and I was forever changed. I met a family I never knew I had, friends and a culture that has shaped who I have become. I only had Maisie for nineteen years of my life, but I don't think a hundred years would have been enough.

90. There are 90 million reasons why she came to America, and why she missed Galway. They are the reasons why she was the smartest woman

I have ever known. They are some of the reasons why she was brave, funny, and kind.

Hopefully, you will make some connections in your own life. Allow yourself to feel more emotions and let go of negativity. Watch the clouds in the sky or just turn off the phone. Listen to a song and move to it- just a little bit. Living in the moment-it is just the kind of thing Maisie did.

Read this in order or out of order. Each story can exist independently. The same message will come through if you keep your mind open. Live in the moment. Listen to what someone is saying without thinking of a reply. Listen to someone's story from a long time ago and ask questions. Try to understand someone else's perspective instead of just dismissing it.

Be kind to others-you never know what they are going through. By doing so, your heart will be full when you lay your head on the pillow. Have fun, and always laugh. Share what you feel and be who you are without fear.

There are countless lessons that Maisie taught me. Both of my grand-fathers and grandmothers, my parents, my godmother, aunts, uncles, and great aunts and uncles have taught me so many valuable life lessons. Here are just a few of them.

MAISIE-
THE NEWS

I stared at the letter on the table. I was not sure what to make of it. Should I just throw it out? Was I really considering this? I had thought about it for some time but going to another country was a massive step. I felt overwhelmed and the room was warm all of sudden. I still had a bit of time before I had to tell them anything yet. Nothing was definite. I was hopeful and sad. It was not something I could explain to anyone.

"What are you looking at Maisie?" Michael went to snatch the letter from the table. Michael was interested in everything that had nothing to do with him. He could just be so annoying sometimes. I mean I loved him-he was my brother. He could get on your nerves though.

"Is it for you?" I snapped. As soon as I heard the tone of my own voice, I regretted it. "I don't think so because it would have been addressed to you." I stuffed the letter into my pocket.

"I was only messing. Must be something serious then so." He said in a sarcastic voice. His brown hair fell on his forehead. He was taller than myself and I was tall for a girl. Dad always reminded me that I was the tallest girl he ever knew. Mam was a foot shorter than me. I took after Dad with my height. Sometimes it was just hard because he was the oldest son in the family. I was a woman, and I was meant to be cooking, cleaning, and having babies.

He was shocked, as I never snap at him. He went and sat in the chair facing me. He looked as if he were a little boy that was scolded at school by the teacher. He had his hands folded slouching in the chair. He looked like a small child that was waiting for me to explain what had just happened between us.

"Honestly, you have no privacy here at all." I said frustrated. They were always at me, trying to get me upset. That was the nature of boys, there was nothing you could do with them.

We sat in silence for what seemed like an eternity. I wanted to go into town anyway and get a few bits for the dinner. He had me so twisted that I didn't know what to say.

"So, what does it say?" He smiled as if he knew. He was not going to let this go. He sat up in the chair, his shirt partly untucked. He was also the quickest to move on from an argument. He never stayed upset.

"It still says that it is none of your business." I had him there. He could not have a go at me if he did not know what it was about.

"Must be a letter from Paddy Sullivan up the road." He was delighted with himself. He clapped his hands with victory. I saw his shoulders rise and his chest bursting with pride. Here he was thinking here he had it all figured out. He was always going at me about Paddy Sullivan. Paddy Sullivan is not really my cup of tea. I know well Paddy has his cap set on me. I wasn't interested in being Mrs. Sullivan.

Michael thinks that he knows everything. I would burst his bubble yet. "Well, if you must know, it's a letter from Aunt Honora in New York." I was relieved to have said it aloud. Plus, I did not want that nonsense about Paddy Sullivan getting around.

"Is she coming back for a visit?" Josie yelled. I did not even realize my sister could hear us from the other room. Josie had no problem putting herself in a situation that had nothing to do with her as well. They could have been twins that way. This is what I had been worried about the whole time. Even though they annoyed the head o'me, I still loved them all very much. Mam, Dad, Josie, Annie, Michael, Tommy, Patrick, and Kitty.

Josie and Annie now paraded into the kitchen as if some world news had broken. Josie always looked glamorous no matter what she was at. Her hair was the most perfect brown and pinned back without a strand out of place. She was so slim and that made her look taller. Annie was definitely the shortest of all of us. She had beautiful striking eyes and was always happy and laughing. It was great to be around her as she would always make you feel better.

Josie would make this situation worse than it had to be. Josie could have been in a play with William Shakespeare. God she was so dramatic. She starts waving her arms, collapsing into chairs, and fainting. None of that nonsense was real or necessary. Then I saw Tommy, Kitty and Patrick enter the kitchen. I knew it was all about to come out and I was terrified and relieved.

"No, Aunt Hanora isn't coming back." I said unsure what to say next. How could I tell them I was leaving? That I was not coming back. I wanted to have a little social party as well. I had to tell them, or I would never be able to organize it.

"Maisie, just tell us." Annie had both hands on the table as if the table were holding her up. Annie was my little sister. We had a strong connection where we could speak to each other without words. Something would happen and we would both look at each other and laugh hysterically. Not a word would be said. We knew exactly how the other was going to say or feel before they did.

"Ok, look there is no easy way to say this. I am going to go to America for a year or so." The room was filled with uneasiness. I don't even think anyone was breathing.

All of them came round the table. They stared at me for what seemed like a thousand years.

"What in the name of...." Tommy's voice trailed off. Tommy would be hurt the most. He was always trying to keep the family together. He was always organizing things and planning, so we were all together. He was the one to be suggesting and even organizing dinners.

"America." Josie's tone said it all. They were in shock.

"Yes, I am not going forever. I just want to make some money and see what it is like." I kept emphasizing the fact that I was not going forever. It made it feel like a vacation of sorts. Plus, I would always come back and visit. I could come for long summer trips and at the holidays.

"When will you come back? You would hardly get on a boat again. Once is enough." Kitty, who was always the quiet one, looked at the others.

"Yes, I will come back. I hope to come back as soon as possible. The journey is not as bad as it was. It isn't like a coffin ship anymore. Loads of people have been telling me." Did I even believe that statement? Or was I just saying it to make everyone including myself feel better?

"Wait, have you told others before you told us?" Annie was getting upset I could tell. She was younger than me. Her lovely reddish hair was shining as the light came in through the window.

"No, I haven't told anyone. I just heard a few conversations, outside at Mass." I really had not told anyone.

Mam and Dad came in from the shed. All our faces said that something would never be the same.

We all just looked at each other. Then everyone looked at me at the same time. Mam finally asked what was going on.

"Why are you all standing around like that? Like you seen a ghost?" Dad was laughing trying to break the tension in the room.

"Which one of you is having a baby? God Almighty Michael, what did I tell you about that Bernadette? Her family is a bunch of gypsies and travelers….. I am not able for this now." Mam held onto the door frame and Michael brought her a chair. Mam could get terribly upset, and she did not take time to really understand what was happening. She would get some idea in her head and then assume it must be true.

"No, Mam. You have no faith in me at all. The lot of you." Michael said, tapping his hand on the table. It is Maisie. She has something she wants to tell you." Michael mouthed the word "Sorry." I had no choice now.

"Maisie, spit it out, my nerves are no good. Ah, please, will someone tell me what is going on." She put her head down and braced for the news, holding onto the chair for dear life.

"I was thinking of going to America, to New York." I said it. Silence. I continued talking. "For a short time, I don't even know how long. Aunt Honora said she has a job working in as a housekeeper for the priests. It is some place called Yonkers that she is meant to get a job in. Something like that anyway. She is setting it up, and I would be coming back at some stage. I could also visit, and you could come out if you wanted."

More silence. I swear I heard a mouse scoot across the floor and out to the shed. It was that quiet. My mother was a smaller woman with jet black hair. She had a part in the middle, and it was pulled into a low bun. She always had a shall around her shoulder because she felt a chill. Mam always looked like she was far off. She was plagued with thoughts and faces. People said she was touched and a bit insane, but she had a gift. The spirits spoke to her. She did not know how to handle it and then there was the religious part of it.

"Maisie, you gave me an awful fright. I thought you were with child or dying…." She held onto her chest as if she were holding her heart from falling out of her body. She looked up with tears in her eyes.

"I am sorry about that." I didn't know what to say. I went and knelt beside her to hold her hand.

"You always want your children to have more in life than you did. I could not be happier for you. Although as a mother I will miss you. So, you will have to come back." She said, putting her face in her hands.

"It isn't the worst that can happen." Mam said releasing her grip.

"You know I will be back. There are planes and soon we will all be able to ride on them. Not just the rich folk." I said, holding her arm.

"Yes, love. I don't want you worrying about it." She got up wiping her tears.

"I just want you to know that I will miss all of you very much." I said looking around the room.

"Well, we best be getting something together. Your wake. Maisie- have you heard of this now. You have what's called an Irish wake. All your friends and family get together and wish you the best of luck." Josie said.

"Like a wake as in funeral?" I asked, horrified.

"Well....because some people don't come back. Not everyone can come back." Annie realized she had said too much.

"It is really a great idea. I mean it. And I will be back." I smiled, thankful that they understood.

"Come on now. Those cows are not going to feed themselves." Dad herded us all toward the back door, ironically just like the cows. The hardest part was over. At least I thought it was.

MAISIE-
THE WAKE

It wasn't really a wake, like in the traditional wake. It was a chance for everyone to say goodbye to me, just in case. Just in case I didn't come back from the States. I didn't like that it was being called "The Wake," it all felt a bit too frightening.

"Now, what time are we havin' people over?" Michael asked. He was bringing some bits back from the shop.

"About six or so? Don't be tellin all the lads to come 'ere for the free drink?" I was going to keep it as nice as I could. It was my wake.

"Ah, they'll be grand. Don't be worrying Maisie." Michael was putting his coat on.

I had to get everything ready. Yes, even though it was my party, I had to get it all sorted me self. I had food and drink, and Annie made a few decorations to put around the house. She even made an American flag. She was incredibly good. Even though she was so sad, she still tried to make me happy.

People started arriving about half six. Mom and Dad said they would hang around for a bit, and then leave us alone. They said they didn't want to be around if things got crazy.

I couldn't believe this was happening. I was leaving.

Agnes arrived first with Clare. Agnes and Clare had been my friends since we were little. Agnes was our leader. She made the decisions and organized whatever we were doing.

Clare and Agnes were the best friends one could ever have. Agnes and I were the ones going to the States. It felt like we were leaving Clare behind. We had asked her loads of times to come with us, but she loved Eoghan. It was at the dance hall one night that we realized it.

"Clare, do you hear me talking to you?" I asked, realizing she wasn't paying attention to me.

"Yes, I am listening." She never turned her eyes to me. She was looking at something that was like the Blessed Mother appearing in the middle of the sitting room.

That is when I saw Eoghan across the room. He was laughing with his friends.

"Clare." She finally broke her gaze.

"Someone has a bit of a…" I didn't get to finish.

"Fancy….." Agnes erupted in laughter. She danced around Clare as if it were a celebration.

"You wouldn't dare." Clare already knew what Agnes was thinking. She would talk to the boys all the time, not like myself and Clare.

But back then, Agnes went up to Eoghan. She called Clare over to chat to him and they were together ever since. It was all down to Agnes.

I couldn't believe that we were all sitting here in my house, and I was leaving in the morning.

Myself, Agnes, and Clare sat round the table. I felt so torn. I was delighted to be going-but I was about to start a new life. I would not be seeing me friends or me family.

"Well now what do you reckon Maisie? Will ya be suited to marry a Yank? A tall dark and handsome man will be your knight in shining armor." Clare was laughing away. I knew she was just messing, and she would miss me.

"No, I won't be getting married." I told them. They looked at each other with surprise and then disbelief.

"Maisie, you don't have to worry about the little things like what love is supposed to look like. It is different in New York. We seen what you put down as the height as well on the passport there. The only time you were 5 foot 5 was when you were about twelve." They were filling up my glass at the same time.

"Well, to be honest, I just that I don't want men to be thinking they should be worrying that I am taller." I knew men didn't like it that I was taller than them, especially the brothers. They were always taking the mick.

"Ah, we are only getting a rise out of you." They lifted their drinks signaling me to take another sip.

Was this the last time I would be home? God I was filled with so many emotions. John had come over to us and sat down.

"The States. God, I can only imagine what you will be getting up to there. Sure, I might come out there to you there now." John was so kind; he was a good friend of Agnes and myself.

"That would be great, what are you thinking of doing?" Agnes asked.

"Bit o' labour." He said, pressing his hair down on the top of his head.

"That's grand, it would be so nice to have some we knew from home over there." I said and realized that John was looking right into my eyes. What was that about? The look lasted longer than it should.

"Yeah, I was thinking. It might be time to set up a life for meself." He said smiling. Then he winked and tilted his head as if to signal to me that I should know what he meant.

John was lovely and kind. He was a good man, but I don't think we would be a good match. The rest of the evening John was around me every time I turned around. I didn't want to assume, but I was right that he had his eye on me. How was I going to handle this? It wasn't as if he were coming on the boat with me. There would be loads of time to sort it out.

It was then that Mrs. McGovern came into the house. We weren't sure if she would come. She was able to connect with the spirits. She would do your fortune if you believed in it. I knew the only one in charge of my fate was God. She wasn't really invited to the parties, she just landed at them.

Michael went to the front door and welcomed her into the house. She always had a shawl on, no matter the temperature. She was in shades of red and black tonight. Agnes called her "The White Witch," because of her long braided white hair and pale complexion. The young ones pointed and laughed at her if she was passing in the street. I never really spoke to the woman. Sometimes she would sit outside the butcher on a tiny stool. She would have a little mug with a few pence in it. Patrick would ask her which horse to bet on. She would just give him the Evil Eye, knowing he was taking the mick.

Kathleen O'Reilly said she was spot on in her predictions. The White Witch told her that she would marry Paddy Donnellan on the fifth of the fifth and they would have five children. Of course, now she was only having the second baby, but Kathleen reckons it will happen.

"Maisie, I have come to tell you your fortune." She said and looked up to the ceiling as if she were getting some sign just as she was saying it.

"Well, what harm anyway?" I sat down at the table, and she followed.

She gestured for me to give over my hands. She studied them looking both relieved and concerned. I wasn't bothered at all; it was a bit o entertainment.

"A piece of silver must cross my palm." She was looking for money as usual.

"I have it." Tommy yelled from across the room. He came over and placed it into her hands.

"Now." She said about to get started.

The room was so quiet you could hear the wind howling outside. I got a chill up my spine, but it wasn't from that now. I was pure frightened. I took one of my hands back and lifted the whiskey to my lips. It burned my throat but not in a bad way.

"Maisie, I see a death, but not like a person-more like someone changing their life." She said looking past us.

It was the wake; I mean that really wasn't anything shocking.

"Well, what do you see for marriage and a home?" I asked really wondering about both.

"Two little girls. I see a husband and the letter M stands out. It just keeps showing me the word heart." She looked at the wall, but it looked like she was looking much farther into the world.

"At least I am getting married." I said, making a smirk to Patrick.

"Something with the heart, I keep seeing a heart." She looked out past us.

"Are you sure you didn't meet anyone?" Josie asked, smiling.

"I didn't meet anyone, sure why would I be going if I found love here?" I was getting annoyed at this stage.

"Well, I can only tell you what I see. I see a lot of girls as well." She said as if she were checking with someone.

"Time will tell then." I wasn't sure what would happen next.

"Josie, I am moving on to yourself now. Now, I see the initial "J" coming through. Does that mean anything to ye?" she asked.

"No, I haven't a clue as to what you were talking about." She suddenly looked uncomfortable. I had no idea why.

"Annie, I can see the letter "B," but it is some sort of a nickname." Annie shrugged her shoulders and looked at me. "You will have a fair amount of land as well. I see the rows and a large family. You will meet your husband in a few weeks."

We just took in the information. None of it really meant anything to us. Mrs. McGovern had been right before about many things. She also just likes to come to parties and have a few drinks.

Friends started leaving and everyone reminded me that the train was leaving early in the morning. I looked around and wondered who I would see again after I left. Would I see everyone again? It was too much to handle. I felt the tears but fought them off.

MAISIE-
THE DAY I HAD TO LEAVE

Josie, Kitty, Michael, Tommy, Patrick, and Annie were all still sleeping. We had been up all hours into the night. And there is no way that Mam and Dad got any sleep either. The singing and dancing with all of us together was just what I needed. I carefully got dressed so as not to wake them up. I was so excited that the day was here. I wrapped a sweater around my shoulders. It was chilly even for September. I hurried downstairs to light the fire.

As I stepped down onto the landing, the smell of ale and cigarettes was like a punch in the face. There were even a few of Michael's friends asleep on the sofas. I gathered a few glasses carefully and brought them to the sink. I opened the back door to give the place a bit of air. The wind gust blew past me and down the hallway. It wasn't exactly great boat weather. The turf was in the wagon, so I grabbed a few sods and went back into the sitting room.

When the fire finally started to go, I stayed a few minutes there to warm up. I imagined that the boat was going to be quite cold. I had heard many stories about how loved ones didn't "make" the journey. This was a chance I was willing to take.

I looked around the room to try to figure out where to begin cleaning. The place was in some state. I picked up some plates and the silver would need to be polished after it was washed.

"Need some help?" Annie startled me in the kitchen.

"God almighty, you frightened the life out of me." I leaned my hand on the edge of the counter for support.

"Oh, I am sorry Maisie, I thought you heard me." She said, throwing her arms around my waist.

I still couldn't believe this was happening.

"That was some night there last night." I was still a bit tired.

"It was quite fun actually. I can't believe…" Her voice trailed off.

"It's okay. I am sure I will be back. You'll see." I said trying to convince myself.

"I hope so." Annie said. She began picking up glasses and plates then placing them into the sink.

Michael came from the back room scratching his curly, brown hair. He collapsed into a kitchen chair.

"Jaysus. Is it morning already?" His voice was cracking.

"You didn't have a care in the world last night." Annie said as she smacked his shoulder with a dishtowel.

"Go on and leave me be. Do you not feel sorry for me?" He put his hands behind his head and leaned back in the chair.

"Oh, we do. You poor thing." I said sarcastically. Annie began washing the dishes and I dried them. After a few minutes she said what I had been waiting for someone to say to me, "Maisie, you will be fine out there. Out of all of us, you will be the one who would make it." She said putting the plates down to turn to me.

"Hopefully, I am nervous about being sick the whole time. I am dreading the boat. I have heard nightmare stories about it." I wasn't sure right now if I was doing the right thing.

"You'll be grand. This time in a fortnight-you will be seeing herself." Annie looked up at the ceiling and I couldn't imagine what she was on about.

"Aunt Margaret's apartment? I don't think the building is that high now. Sure, why are you looking at the sky?" I asked.

"No, Lady Liberty." She took a deep breath and still stared at the ceiling as if it was the world.

"Oh, I know now what you mean. Yes, it will be some sight." I smiled and then hugged Annie. The sadness came over me.

"We had better be off." Dad came from the back of the house. "The train doesn't wait for you. It is a long journey."

"Mam is in bed." Josie came out from the back bedroom. "Go in and see her."

She was laying facing the wall. I am sure she heard the door creak when I came in, but she didn't move. Mam wasn't always feeling her best. The doctor called it a case of the "nerves." No one could explain why some people got the nerves and others did not. I didn't know if I would have them. The onset was usually after the change of life.

"Maisie, is that yourself? I am just not great today. It has got nothin to do with you leavin and I will be in bed today anyway. I don't want you to leave thinking you are causing the nerves. I will be okay." She sat up in bed and outstretched her arms. She looked so small in the bed. She was so small beside me.

"Come 'ere to me now lovine." She hugged me so tightly. I wanted to stop her and tell her I wouldn't go. I wanted her to tell me that I should stay with her.

"Mam…" I said before I could finish.

"We will all be fine now love. Don't you be worrying. They are talking about airplanes and all. You will be back. I will send Josie over in a few months to ye. Sure, you'll be with Aunt Hanora, and she will look afta you." She brushed the hair from my brow to behind my ears.

"I don't…." I said and she cuddled me one more time before another word was said.

The truth is I realized at that moment that I could go back. If I believed in my dream to go to New York, I could believe in coming back home.

We cried for what seemed like ages. I couldn't think of what to say or do.

"I guess this is it." I said not believing it. Mom didn't come down to the train. She was terribly upset. When I realized that she wasn't coming, I thought about cancelling the whole thing.

"I guess so." I said as Michael hugged me first. Patrick was next, then Annie. Kitty, Josie, and Tommy were last.

"Take care of yourself now Maisie. Come back to us, even if it is just for a visit." Dad choked back tears.

"I'll come back. You know I will." I wasn't sure if that was true though.

I boarded the train and went to find a seat. It was fairly packed to be honest, more than I thought.

I chose a seat by the window and put my one case by my feet. I had only been on a train once in me life. I looked around to see if anyone was watching me. I didn't want to look like I didn't know what I was doing.

A gentleman with light brown hair looked at the paper in his hand and then at the numbers for the seats. He smiled and said, "Now, seems I am just across from you. I am James Nolan." He also tipped his hat to me.

"Nice to meet you James, I am Maisie-well Mary." I had to remember that Maisie was me nickname.

"Lovely to meet you as well. Are you headed for Queenstown; I mean Cobh?" He said lifting his suitcase to the luggage shelf above us. He gestured that I should give him my case as well.

"Thank you, that would be great. I am heading to Cobh to join the SS Munchen to New York." I handed him the case. This was nice I could have someone to talk to on the way there. This whole journey would be exhausting.

"I am headed as well. I am on the same boat, and it is said to be quite a journey from what I have heard. I am meeting up with one of my good friends, Agnes. She has family down in Cork." I was desperate for anyone to disagree with me and say that it wasn't as bad as people said.

"I am not looking forward to that now either." He said gesturing fear in his face.

"I heard it can take us up to ten days, depending on the wind." I wanted to change the subject because I didn't want to think about how sick we might be.

"Yes, I heard that alright." He nodded. He took out a small booklet that was a prayer book. Most of the pages were dog-eared and the book looked like it had been given to him by an uncle or something.

"Are you from Ireland?" I asked him while he thumbed through the book.

"No, I was born in a place called the Bronx. There are loads of Irish people there. You will see, where are you headed?" He said putting the book next to him to give me his attention.

"I am going to be working with my aunt Honora. She is working with the Church and knows of another parish that needs someone to help in the rectory. It is cooking and cleaning." I said proudly.

"That sounds nice, and will you go back?" he asked. I saw him look down as if he asked too much. "Well, I go back and forth. The journey isn't pleasant, but I like to see my family." He said hoping to not upset me.

'Will I go back?' This was a question to which there was no genuine answer.

"Perhaps, at some stage." I said not believing it myself.

"I am sure you will go back. Technology is really advancing." He said wanting to help as he saw the sadness all over my face.

"Yes, that is true." I responded feeling a bit more positive.

"The Lord says that as long as we believe in Him, we will always be at peace." He said looking up.

"Are you a priest?" I asked.

"I've been called by our Lord." He said with certainty and pride. "At the moment I am studying at a place called Dunwoodie in a place called Yonkers.

"That is where my Aunty is from." I couldn't believe it was the same place.

"Is that right?" He said delightedly.

"I am going to be in Yonkers for a few days and then I have to go down to the city to a Church called 'Sacred Heart.' Are you familiar?" I asked.

"Yes, I know the parish priest there, Father Michael." He said as he closed his jacket. "You are in good hands."

"Isn't it a small world?" I answered almost not believing my luck.

"Yes, and God does everything for a reason. We just must try to figure out all the things God has planned for us. He planned for us to meet today. You were worrying about the journey. Now we are chatting, and you seem less worried." He said looking out the window.

Where did this man come from? He was so young too. He already had the call.

"It is true. I never thought of it like that." I was stunned. I always welcomed God in my life. After meeting Father Nolan, I realized God is everywhere and my faith in Him will get me through this tough time.

"That is beautiful. Thank you for sharing that with me." I added.

"You saw that yourself. I only helped you look at things more openly." He responded. He was an incredibly wise man. I was so happy to have met him. I hoped we would become friends.

"Sounds like the train is getting started." I was delighted and saddened. It was hard to understand my feelings.

"Time will go by very quickly. You will see." He said then looked out the window.

I was terrified. Terrified that I was making the biggest mistake of my life. Terrified, I might never see my parents again. I also knew that I had to leave, or I might never have a chance of happiness.

I took some deep breaths and repeated the words he said over and over. He had already reassured me; well, I reassured myself.

Maisie-
2876 miles

"2876 miles. That's what I heard your man say." I insisted, but Agnes didn't believe it was that far. When I was getting on the boat, I asked the man collecting the tickets how far New York was.

"How could it be that many miles?" She rolled her eyes at me as if I didn't understand what she said.

"Suit yourself." I said to her, knowing there was no changing her mind. It was myself and Agnes that were about to change our lives forever. We made it to Cobh.

"Once we get on board, we can drop the cases into the room. Then we can go off and explore. My friend Tommy is meant to be on board. Tommy O'Neill, I know him from town." Agnes had never been on a boat, but you would never know that based on how she behaved.

"Let's get on the queue now." I said not believing all this was happening. I was relieved that she was here. I didn't feel so scared.

Agnes was one of my dearest friends. We had been friends since primary school. I had never seen her before the day she came up to me at Church. She was tall and had beautiful blond curls tied up in pigtails. Her hair was still brilliant blond-haired person. My hair was light, but not shiny like hers. It was a mix of blond and brown. I was sure I was average looking. My mam didn't have time to tell me I was beautiful

My mother had seven children. I don't remember a time when Mam wasn't pregnant. There were also pregnancies that ended before they should have. There were two that I can remember. I was the oldest. It was when I started to understand things.

One day Agnes and I were walking to school. She was kicking stones and making clouds of smoke.

"What would they do if we didn't go?" she asked.

"Go where?" I asked.

"To school…silly. I mean we can mitch." She said amusingly.

"We couldn't do that now." I said with authority.

"Why? What can they really do to us?" She asked walking in front of me backwards.

"We could get thrown out or punished." I said as if I were scolding her. Sometimes I felt as if I were the mother.

"They can't do that anymore. Kids have to get an education." She said nodding.

"Well then, that is the perfect reason to go." I said walking a bit faster.

"Maisie is a scaredy cat." She said laughing. Agnes could make you so aggravated.

"Fine. Let us not go then." I was terrified. I had never skipped school unless I was extremely sick. I wasn't going to let this one tell me I was afraid.

"That's what I mean." She grabbed my hand and we started running toward the Abbey. We arrived at this magnificent oak tree. It looked easy enough to climb and there was an apple I spotted.

"Maisie-you are a young lady; you shouldn't be climbing trees." she said rolling her eyes and laughing hysterically. We were delighted with ourselves.

I paid no mind to her and started climbing. I locked my foot into a groove in the tree. Looking up I saw another apple a small bit higher. I would try for that one. I might even bring a few back for the boys. Tommy and Mikey loved apples. At that moment I heard a snap. I grabbed on for dear life onto one of the branches. The one branch under me foot snapped. I tried to lock my foot into another groove but was unsuccessful. I hit several branches that scraped the sides of me arms. All those thoughts in about 3 seconds, until I hit the cold, hard ground. The branch wasn't the only thing that snapped that day.

Agnes said I let out a scream that she was sure they heard in Donegal.

"Maisie, are you hurt?" She said looking me over.

"Me arm, it is on fire. I want to rip it off. Look at the state of me wrist….." I realized what had happened. I had broken my wrist.

"You'll have to see the doctor." She was shaking her head.

"I will be fine. It is no problem.

I held out for a few days, but the pain was fierce. It wasn't until Mam asked me to carry the dishes into the kitchen. I tried holding one plate with my broken arm and it fell onto the table again.

"Jesus, Mary and Joseph." Mam didn't have to say anything else. I was in for it now.

"Mam, I just hurt it a bit. It'll be grand." I knew it wasn't going to be fine.

"What happened to ye, let's have a look?" She was coming toward me.

"It's no bother, I swear." I said as I darted into the other room.

"Mary Ann Burke." Mam said. She didn't have to use verbs; her tone made the words themselves action words.

It was broken. Mam was livid.

Eventually sometime after that experience, we stopped going to school. We had chores and had to help at home. It wasn't just our families that stopped us from going to school, everyone just stopped going. Agnes still talked about leaving. She would always look out into the distance when she would talk about the future. We talked about it all the time. I didn't want to leave, but I pretended I did. We were in the field one day; her farm was just beside mine.

"Maisie, they aren't coffin ships anymore. Sure, people will die. But people die every single day. You could die going across the road." She had such a way of looking at things, terrifying and exciting at the same time.

"Are you not scared of never seeing your family again?" I had never imagined leaving my family.

"Not for a second." She said looking to the sky. She took a deep breath. "We could come back. They are talking about airplanes."

Who is they?

Agnes really wanted to get out of Kilconnell. Seamus had broken her heart. She swears it didn't affect her, but I know it did. She fell in love with him. He had met her in our St. Michael's Church Parish Hall at one of the dances. He promised her the world and the next week she saw him with Molly Hayes from Ballinasloe. Molly had told everyone that they were getting married, including my sister Josie. Josie wasn't exactly sensitive when it came to love. Josie just told everyone things- things the way she saw it. I told her not to tell Agnes that piece of information and that I would break it to her. She was devastated. I hadn't seen her for a week, so I called to her house. That was the first time she mentioned the states. I didn't know this magical place she had been talking about was the States.

Now, here we are getting on the ship.

The ship was massive. It was bigger than anything I had ever seen. It must have just had a fresh coat of paint on it because it looked magnificent. It was like a whole town, even a city. People were running around all over the place, some were smiling, and others were crying. I knew we had a few hours of whatever, but it just seemed so hectic. The only thing we ever rushed for was Mass, and that was probably because we had a few too many the night before.

The rooms were organized ahead of time, so we booked in together. I couldn't imagine having to room with a stranger. We have got a small room with two beds; it would have been more like a closet to be honest. Whenever she and I were together, we would make do with what we had. Then it hit me, we were really going to America. I was going today. I had to remember to breathe, or I would get worked up. I didn't need my stomach jumping before the ship left.

"Let's go see what is going on at the top deck, Maisie." Agnes was bursting with excitement.

"Ok, I am right behind ye." I had no idea what to expect.

Out on the deck it was just breathtaking, the air was clear, and I took a deeper breath than I ever had in all my life. Agnes had run over to someone she must have known. Imagine all the way down here in Cobh. I followed her to them. She introduced me, but I was still taking it all in.

A couple standing beside me stood out. The woman had bright blonde hair and huge blue eyes. Her husband did as well, at least I thought it was her husband. I looked for their wedding rings, they didn't put them on. Could you imagine if they were not married and just on the ship as a couple just courting? The woman smiled at me. Then she said something I had never heard before.

"Hallo wie geht's dir. Mein Name ist Katerina." She put out her hand.

I nodded and responded, "Hello."

She looked at me as puzzled as I was, so I just smiled.

"Ah, your one is speaking in German." Agnes took me by the arm.

"Oh, that must be it." I responded. I had forgotten it was a German ship we were on. I was looking forward to meeting new people, but the language was a problem.

We walked into the dining hall. It was a huge hall filled with crystal and shimmering lights. I had not seen anything like it.

"Won't it be great to have dinner here?" I said to Agnes.

"Maisie this is for the first-class passengers." Agnes said.

"Oh, right, that is what I meant. Imagine we could have dinner here?" I tried to recover.

I forgot we were below decks. I forgot that I didn't have enough money for a real ticket. I wanted to forget that type of thing when I got to the states. Hopefully, I will be in New York.

Maisie-
The Journey

I honestly cannot imagine how any of us survived. I know the coffin ships were worse, and well the Titanic is just another thing. Yes, an Irish man built it, but the English man was the one that sunk it.

We were on the ship for about ten days. You could lose track of the sickness. I always felt jumpy in my stomach.

The rooms were small with many beds. Agnes was beside me though, which was helpful because I was so nervous. It was freezing at night as well. We had loads of blankets, but a chill that never left you. I couldn't sleep well either with the rocking of the boat.

I thought I would never stop getting sick. It was just awful. The one woman just down a few rooms died from dehydration. I managed to sip water with a few bits of bread. I honestly prayed to God every single night to help me through it so I could see each morning.

Agnes didn't seem to feel it as much. She said she was queasy and unsettled in her tummy all right, but she wasn't getting sick.

One night I was walking about the deck of the ship. I could see into the dining room; it was like looking into another world. The chandelier was magnificent, and it sparkled around the whole room. I wondered what it was like to have that much money where you could be entertained by others. I didn't necessarily want to be rich, but I wanted to be comfortable. I didn't want to worry about the next meal or have old shoes on. I just wanted to be somewhere in the middle of being poor and wealthy.

I looked down at my old dress. I wouldn't be able to buy anything new when I was in America. I had to send money back to help them at home. They were having a tough time; I couldn't be buying meself a new dress. There was plenty of time for things like that. I had the wonderful opportunity to live in another country and the others stayed behind. I wanted them to get more land and be taken care of. I felt my chest fill with sadness and guilt. It was for the best, I knew that.

I looked around the deck and saw Father Nolan.

"Hello Maisie. How are you keeping?" He asked, rubbing his hands together for warmth. He had such a powerful presence.

"I am so sick." I said, taking a deep breath.

"Well, I must say this boat doesn't agree with me." He said, placing his hand over his stomach.

"How many more days?" I said wondering.

"Four," and his voice trailed off. "Maisie, you must think about all the sacrifices that Our Lord went through. Yes, this is difficult, I will not ignore that. It is all about how we look at things. Isn't it? We are lucky to be standing here. I have performed Last Rites to several people on board." He said leaning his hand on the rails.

"You are right. I don't know what you must think of me." I said embarrassed for complaining.

"Maisie, it is understandable. I am simply teaching you the way of our Lord. You are a particularly good person that loves her family. You want to take care of your family there by going to the States and risking everything. I am only trying to help your mind become stronger to survive. Lean on the Lord. Speak to him at night, in your head in the middle of the day or however you like. He is there for you. He will walk with you." James was such an amazing man. I couldn't believe his wisdom.

"I will of course." I said really planning on thinking about his words. "I am going back to my room to get some rest and clear my head. Thank you for your words. They have helped so much."

"Why don't we meet again tomorrow at the same time? I believe I can help you with whatever you are struggling with." He said confidently.

"How did you know I was struggling?" I asked.

"I knew there was something. Let us find a way to have God give you strength?" He put his arm on my shoulder and I felt strength suddenly.

"Yes, that will be great." I said feeling hopeful for the first time.

We met every night around the same time. He told me stories from the Bible, people he had met and lessons he had learned. This experience was really what got me through everything.

I went back to my room and felt as if a huge weight was lifted off me. It didn't seem so dark and frightening. I thought about James telling me about the Statue of Liberty. I couldn't wait to see her. I realized that I must look at things differently. It wasn't this whole journey in front of me. I had already done so many things on my own. I took the train and survived six days on this ship. By changing my thinking, I found strength.

I lay down in bed and my tummy wasn't upset at all. I imagined I had to have lost weight. I was tall so I always weighed more than the girls in my class.

"Big Boned Mary," is what the girls would call me. I would try to respond but Agnes always stood up for me.

"Ya ugly hoor." Agnes screamed this one time. The girl looked at me and then turned around to run. I wish I were like Agnes.

I remember my eyes widened bigger than I could have imagined they would be able to. Agnes had no fear whatsoever.

I smiled and felt my eyes get heavier. I began the rosary in me head. I imagine I only made it about four or five into the decade of the rosary and I was asleep.

Maisie-
And there She was....

I had known we were getting close. Everyone was talking about it. We would see her in a couple of minutes or so. I tried to imagine what she would look like. I really had nothing to compare it to.

I was getting some air up on the deck. It was so windy up there. I liked feeling the wind blowing my hair. I always had my hair pinned because that is how a lady wore her hair. I haven't seen Agnes since this morning. She was always making friends wherever she went. She never left me out of her socializing and chatting- she always asked if I wanted to join her and her new friends.

I just wanted to get there-New York. I needed to get off the boat and make my way to find Aunt Hanora. She was taking me and Agnes to the apartment. I just wanted a warm dry bed.

I also heard the weather in New York was still warm. Imagine September being hot. I was worried about the weather differences. New York winters were brutal and freezing. There were things called blizzards as well. In 1920, they had a huge storm in February of that year. It was seventeen inches of snow. Annie and I read about it in the paper. We took out a measuring tape and put it on the floor to see where the snow would be up to on our bodies. It was just at my knees and past Annie's knees.

"God Almighty, that would be very hard to walk through." I said to Annie.

"It wouldn't be my cup of tea." Annie said with a chill up her spine.

The most snow Ireland ever saw was about three inches or so. It never stuck either-to make a snowman or snowballs. The country wasn't made for snow. I remember one Christmas Eve it started snowing and it was so beautiful. It just covered the ground like a cozy white blanket. It even decorated the trees so nicely as well.

That was something I wasn't used to. The dampness of Ireland was bad enough, but it wasn't ever as cold at home. I also heard that New York summers could reach 37 degrees Celsius. I had never felt the temperature that hot. I am sure you would be burning your feet at the beach with that temperature. I would also be burned badly on account of my pale skin.

I had a lot to look forward to and experience. I was either bursting with excitement or overcome by sadness. Father Nolan was doing his rounds on the ship and stopped to chat to me.

"Almost there, about ten minutes give or take." He said looking out into the distance.

"Wait-as in the Statue?" I felt I would burst with excitement.

"Yes, it is wonderful to see how much better you are." Father Nolan was so kind.

"I am much more hopeful. Thanks be to God." I said very relieved.

"God will lead you where you need to go." He said, placing his hand on my shoulder.

"Father, I couldn't have done this without our talks." I said so thankfully. "We will have to meet up in New York."

"You couldn't have done this without God." he said nodding his head. "Yes, I don't see why not. I can show you around my church."

I looked into his eyes for a moment. He was looking beyond me in the distance. He drew in a long deep breath.

"It is time to turn around Maisie." He said pointing behind me. I was puzzled. Were we going to pray or just take in the quiet? That is when I hear someone scream with delight.

Lady Liberty. She was magnificent. She stood taller than anything I could have even imagined. She was bright and strong. She represented everything I dreamed about. It was like a dream, and I didn't want anyone to wake me up.

I never thought I could do anything like this. I had no education since fifth class, and I was about thirteen. Now, here I am going to New York! Father Nolan was telling me the story about Lady Liberty. I couldn't even hear him. It was like I was in a wind tunnel. I was so excited that I was afraid I would faint.

"Isn't that fascin-Maisie, are you listening to me?" Father Nolan put his hand on my arm, and I broke out of the trance.

"Sorry Father, I am just feeling overwhelmed." I took a deep breath.

"Yes, I imagine you would be." He said smiling.

We had to circle around her for a bit. The ship had to anchor and fit in some sort of slot. The boat began to dock. Father Nolan handed me an address and smiled as if he were proud of me.

"Don't be a stranger now." He said, tipping his hat. "God is always with you even when you are alone."

I watched the workers run with ropes around the boat. There was also a great deal of yelling amongst them. I could see American soil. It was unreal. When the landing came down, we watched many health officers board the ship. They seemed to only be looking at the first-class passengers who were on deck beside me and Father Nolan.

We made our way out of the area. We weren't first-class passengers; we had been up doing our permitted walk on the deck.

"Maisie- I was fortunate to meet you. I have a feeling this is the beginning of a beautiful friendship." He said, taking a deep breath.

"As am I fortunate to meet ye." I said smiling. "I will definitely call to ye."

I took a deep breath and went looking for Agnes.

MAISIE-
WHATEVER YOU DO, DON'T COUGH

Leaving the ship gave me a feeling that I had never experienced before. The relief that I survived, and the promise of New York were unforgettable and incomparable to anything. Walking on the dock we walked beside our baggage as they moved across the sliding staircase made me feel famous. I was like a movie star arriving at an award show.

"Whatever you do, don't sneeze or cough." Agnes said bending down to adjust to the bottom of her case.

"I have to hold it in you mean?" I was so confused. I had done it before, but there was always a noise when it went through your ears.

I stood in a very long line with Agnes. The journey was taking forever. I looked up and saw a magnificent ceiling. It was a bigger room than I had ever been in my life.

"Wait, why can't I cough?" I really was confused.

"You will get stopped and seen as a sick one." Agnes was talking but her lips were barely moving.

"All right, no worries." I said, but it was all I could think about. Then I felt my nose itch as it usually does when you are thinking about it.

"Step forward Miss…." The gentleman's voice trailed off as he waited for Agnes' passport. He was a large man, with broad shoulders. He was born in the States.

I couldn't believe how loud it was in this room. I waited for my turn. The truth was I wanted to run, run as fast as I could to meet my aunt.

In the queue there were women and children, men were on the other end of this gigantic room. The children looked so tired, as if they hadn't properly slept in a lifetime. Kids were resilient though and would land back on their feet. I was thinking as if I were an old woman.

The children smiled and I found strength to move. One little boy waved at me. I waved back and he smiled. The journey was so hard on the children.

Another gentleman waved me forward. All I could think about was coughing. I tried to think about anything else. I took a deep breath and stepped forward.

"Passport and name please." He said very solemnly.

"Mary Anne Burke." I said as I handed him the passport.

"What is your business in the States?" He said looking into my eyes.

"I am afraid I do not have a business." I said hearing my voice shake.

"What are your plans for how you will earn a living in the states?" He said looking through my passport pages. He raised his eyebrows. He looked up waiting for me to respond.

"I will be living with my aunt, and hopefully get a job cleaning in a church or rectory." I was hoping that was what he meant.

"Do you have any sicknesses you want to mention before you see the doctor? It is better to be upfront about it?" He closed the passport and handed it back to me.

"No, no illnesses." I waited to see what was next.

"Straight through this way." He led me to a room with tall slim doors that reached heaven.

The walls were a dull gray color. My stomach felt strange, I had hoped it was just nerves. How could I even prepare for this? Then I took a deep breath. It was all I could do to prevent myself from passing out.

"Good morning, and welcome to New York." A short, bald man entered the room. He had a white coat buttoned all the way up to his neck. He looked European if I had to guess. He spoke very slowly. I wondered how many years he must have been in school to do this job.

"Good morning." I knew that I should say as little as possible.

"Now, we can get started. I am going to examine you for a number of diseases" he said looking at me from the top of my head to the toes on my feet.

"That is fine." I said knowing I really had no choice.

"I will be testing you for trachoma, tuberculosis, diphtheria, and other poor states of health such as poor physique, pregnancy, and mental disability." It was like he was reading them off a piece of paper.

"Ok." It was getting hot in that room. I took long deep breaths. What if I had a disease? Would I go back on the boat? Did he say pregnancy? I am not even married. This was going to be a long exam and I was terrified.

The doctor looked me up and down. I looked around and at your man's shoes. They were black and like boots with laces tied tightly and very shiny as if he polished them a minute ago.

I remembered someone told me that they write on you while you are here. Agnes had a cousin that told her that in a letter. Each symbol represented something, what he had just said that I didn't understand. They all had writing on their shoulders and back. It was like a white crayon or something. It was letters like EX, C, S or X.

"Any sickness?" He asked while he was examining me.

"No, thank God." I said, taking a breath.

"How did you feel on the boat?" He asked looking me straight in the eye.

"Well, not great to be honest. The sea was rough enough. Many of us were sick to the stomach most of the time." I said instantly regretting it.

"Yes, that is to be expected. It can be rough." He said continuing to write on the paper. He had no real expression.

"So, am I getting sent back?" I asked holding back tears. I took several deep breaths.

"No, are you worried about getting sent back?" He asked me as he put the clipboard and the chalk.

"Well, we were told to not say anything if we weren't well on the boat." I felt my shoulders fall. "However, I cannot lie like that."

"Being sick on the boat was to be expected Ms. Burke." He said, placing a mark above my shoulder.

"If you don't mind me asking-what is that mark for?" I figured this was when it was over.

"The arch of your back is a slightly bit off. It may have been from the journey. When you get settled here in New York, you can find a doctor that will have a look at it." He said looking me straight in the eye with a bright light.

"I understand." I took a deep breath and felt relief. I wanted to get out of there.

He felt me throat, neck and looked in my ears. He told me to swallow which was not easy when someone asks you to do it on the spot.

He wrote what seemed like a book on a piece of paper. I was sure he had found something. After an eternity he said, "Well Ms. Burke, I can't see why you can't be admitted." He nodded his head.

"So, I can stay here in New York?" I was shocked. I picked up my handbag and smoothed out my clothes.

"Yes, Welcome to America." Words I never thought I would hear anyone say.

I thought then that we had the all clear. Agnes said that she was sure her cousin said there would be a few more things we had to do. It took forever. It was like years we were there, just waiting. A guard collected us from the medical rooms. Fortunately, myself and Agnes were beside each other during the medical and we finished at the same time.

"I can't believe it?" I said, nearly crying. "Your man said the bit about bein' welcome to America."

"It is absolutely unbelievable

We were led into another room with a huge space and there were pews like at mass. We just sat waiting to be called again. We were called and we had to report to an inspector who was sitting behind a very tall desk. I couldn't believe the questions they asked me. Was I ever convicted of a crime? I didn't even know what the word meant but I figured it was something bad. Someone said there were twenty-nine questions. What in the name of God could they ask about for twenty-nine questions?

"Ms. Burke, who is the President here in America?" He asked, not even looking up from the papers.

"President Harding." I knew it well thanks be to God.

The questions went on and on. Just when I thought I would collapse, the officer said, "Welcome to America," and he stamped my passport and pushed it towards me.

I stood frozen in the spot. It was like I was the only one there.

Maisie, are you okay?" Agnes was beside me showing me her stamp.

"I am now." I opened my passbook and showed her mine. We erupted in laughter and joined arms.

Maisie-
First Hours In New York

After much excitement, myself and Agnes headed over to the Money Exchange and we got our first American dollars. From there we had to collect the luggage and head to a ferry. I couldn't believe we had to go on another boat, but this was much shorter. It took us to what was called Manhattan. It was there that Hanora and her friend met me.

"Maisie, God Almighty I can't believe you are here. This must be Agnes, lovely to meet ya." She hugged me so tight which made me feel so much better. I felt so alone the last few weeks.

"Lovely to meet you too, Aunt Hanora." Agnes was so funny. Agnes had no relation to her. But that is how she was.

"It was quite a journey, that I am glad is over." I realized how tired I was.

Aunt Hanora was taking us to her friend in lower Manhattan to stay for the night. I tried to take in as much as I could, but we were so tired. We arrived at Mary and John's apartment. They were friends of my Aunt Hanora and she said she had done loads of favors for them in the past. They were really lovely. John had parents that had come over from Tipperary many years ago. The apartment was perfect and lovely. They had a claddah on the wall and the St. Bridget's Cross in the kitchen. John's parents always tried to make the food just like it was in Ireland. They had cooked up an Irish meal for us and cozy beds. It was heaven.

The next day I was on to my parish in a neighborhood called Highbridge. Agnes was working in a rich family's house on Long Island and then onto another job.

"Maisie, I can't believe we did it." She said with her eyes filling with tears. I didn't know if she was happy or sad to leave me. I think it was a bit of both.

"Agnes, sure once you are done with the Long Island job you can call into me in the rectory. We are still going to see each other...." I was hoping we would.

"Yes, God Almighty, Maisie we will. Of course, I will write to you and see you soon. I love you so much dear friend." She squeezed me so hard. With that she was off.

I was terrified. The next day Hanora brought me to the Church. She told me she was in a hurry, but she would see me in a few days. I couldn't believe it. I was really on my own.

I stood on the steps and looked at the massive Church. I was working in a Church called Sacred Heart in Highbridge. There was a small sign that hung outside of the main door that read "Rectory" with an arrow pointing to the right.

I knew that was where I had to report and meet the Fathers.

I braved it and knocked on the thick wooden door. I heard barking and couldn't imagine there would be a dog in the rectory. It must be around the corner. The door opened and a tall man with a large dark dog on a leash.

"Hello, you must be Mary. Sorry about Scout here." Father was a tall fella with a strong Cork accent. He wasn't American at all. The dog began jumping up and getting his paws on me coat.

"It is no bother, Father. Yes, lovely to meet you." I stood at the entrance of a large rectory.

"Come in, you must be wrecked from the journey." Father said, ushering me toward a back room that I assumed would be a kitchen.

I walked slowly so I could take it all in. There was a staircase bigger than anything I had ever seen. It had a red patterned carpet on it. I wondered if that went to Church. There were many decorated rooms and a large hallway. The houses and buildings were bigger than anything at home.

I was right that we were headed for the kitchen. It was gorgeous with the brightest yellows and greens. A cabinet displayed handmade China cups and saucers as a decoration. The cups and saucers had little shamrocks on them.

"Ms. Burke, we know you have had quite the journey, but we want you to have something to eat. I am Father John, and this is Father Michael." He said pulling out the chair for me.

I imagined Father John and Father Michael were around the same age. It seemed Father John was from Cork. I wondered where Father Michael was from. If I could just hear him talk for a bit, I would know if he was from Ireland and which county. They both had chestnut brown hair and blue eyes. Father Michael was taller than Father John, but it was Father John that loved his desserts. He wasn't fat, just bigger than the other lad.

"Thank you both so much Fathers." I said putting down my pocket-book and case.

"Ms. Burke, now today we will just give you the lay of the land. We can just give you a tour of the Rectory." Father John said nodding.

"You can call me Maisie. You don't have to call me Ms. Burke. It is too proper." I said smiling.

"Maisie it is then. When you go up the stairs, your room is the first door on the left. It is a small room, but I am sure you will be grand in there." Father Michael said, scratching his head.

"I will be happy no matter what the accommodations are for me. Now, tomorrow I will be able to get started early. What time suits you? Can I start at half five?" I asked looking at both of them.

"Ah no, that is too early. The earliest Mass here is half seven. Father Michael and I do a few masses before we get the breakfast. If that is all right with you" Father John looked at Father Michael for approval as well.

"Yes, all that is fine. I am very easy going so whatever the pair of you need…" I said excited to start.

"Yes, Maisie, we are very easy going as well." Father Michael said.

"Well, I might rest for a while then today. Thank you so much for that. I am still wrecked from the journey." I said getting up to put my dishes on the counter.

"Maisie don't be worrying about that now. Go upstairs and sort yourself. We are grand today with everything. Sure, we will see each other in the morning.

I left the kitchen and headed toward the stairs. I counted and there were fifteen steps. I had never seen more than three or four together. It was amazing. I opened the door to my room. A breeze came through and made the curtain snap back to the glass. The room was large for me because I was always sharing it with my sisters when I was home. There was a lovely duvet covering the bed, a small desk, and a chair. I imagined I would be writing cards or letters to everyone at home there. Life was so different already.

Maisie-
The Day I met Malachy

The doorbell rang and then I realized that I was the one that was supposed to it.

I went out and there was a package on the ground. I carried it in. I went into the office and Father John gestured to me to put it on the table.

"Maisie- we get free samples all the time, help yourself." He said pointing to the mail. He was going through some of the papers that the accountant worked on.

I opened some of the packages. I saw one that had chocolate in a little tin. I secretly loved chocolate. I put them in my pocket and shoved two or three in my mouth. I could sneak them throughout the day.

Father John and Father Michael were so good to me. They let me ease into the jobs they had for me. They were so kind and pleasant. They were telling me that I still needed rest from my journey. The last room they gave me to clean was the accountant's office. I knew it was round the front, but I had never been in it. The accountant had a few days off, so I had not even been introduced. Father John was going over the bits I had to clean in the hallway and the office.

"Maisie, if you could get to the top of the secretary and dust it that would be great. We can't seem to reach it, but if you can't sure it's no worries." Father Michael was saying to me pointing up.

I took one of the chairs and placed it next to the secretary's desk. It was a beautiful desk, dark wood that shined brightly in the room. I stood on the chair with an old rag and wiped the top. It was then I heard the office door open.

I kept tidying the office, cleaning under the desk and inside the drawers. The truth was that I liked to clean and tidy up.

Then, a short, handsome man who I assumed to be the accountant came through the door with his hat on. He saw me and quickly removed it. He was younger than myself and quite stocky, not fat, just bigger.

"I beg your pardon; you must be Mary." He said smiling. "Welcome to Sacred Heart Parish."

"Thanks very much." I said, stepping down from the chair.

"I am Mr. Harte, and I am the accountant here at the Church." He said, nodding his head.

"I am Mary- but sure everyone calls me Maisie." I said not knowing what to say next.

"Maisie, where are you from in Ireland?" He asked.

Father Michael was still there with the rag and the cleaning spray in his hand. I realized that I should say something to him.

"Father Michael, I can have that done now. You have yourself a rest. I will be putting on the dinner in a few." I said taking the cleaning stuff from him.

"That's grand now Maisie." Father Michael hurried out of the room.

"By the way, I am so used to being professional, please call me Malachy." He said as I caught a slight smirk on his face.

"Ok, Malachy it is. Did you ask me a question from before.....what was it?" I asked.

"Where are you from, I am thinking Ireland?" He said, folding his arms and then quickly putting them back to his sides.

"A small village called Kilconnell. Then, that is in Ballinasloe in the County Galway. Have you heard of it?" I asked.

"My family is from Tuam in Galway." He said and I swear he was smiling now.

"You aren't serious, are ya?" I asked so happy to make a connection to home.

"I am indeed." He said. "My parents came here from Ireland when they were young. We have gone back a few times."

He means with his wife. He wasn't wearing a wedding ring though. Why was I worried about this man and whether he was married?

"You mean your wife and your children?" I asked hoping to be wrong. Agnes would have absolutely died laughing at the cheek o' me.

It was then I felt a cramp in me stomach. At first, I thought I was going to be sick. I realized that the pain was much lower.

"Are you okay? You look a little sick." Malachy pulled out a chair.

The doorbell rang but I had to go to the toilet.

"Give me a second, could you just answer the door for me?" I said waving to the door for him to answer it, as I ran down the hall.

I was so sick with the diarrhea. It felt like it never ended. I had not eaten anything unusual, but just the change because I was in another country. People did tell you that your body would have to get used to the water in a new place.

After a while, I headed back to the kitchen. I was going to tell Malachy that I was ill and that I would need to lay down.

Malachy was sitting at the kitchen table having a cup of tea. What would I say to him?

"Maisie, I couldn't help but notice that you look like you are in pain." He said carefully.

"Yes, I have an awful pain I am so embarrassed." I said sitting down.

"What did you eat today?" Malachy asked.

"Nothing out of the usual. I had an egg this morning with the fathers. I had a bit of bread later on. Oh, I also had these chocolates They came in the mail there earlier. I probably just ate too much, and they made my stomach hurt." I placed the tin on the table in front of him.

"You know those aren't chocolate candies. Maisie, those are laxatives." He said waiting for me to have a reaction. I didn't know what he was on about.

"Sorry, that might be an American word. I don't know what that means." I hated that I didn't know every day basic stuff. I was only here a few days and already I felt embarrassed.

"Ah, maybe there is another name for it you use at home. When you cannot go to the bathroom, you could take this, and it is like medicine. They probably have another name-" He stopped when he saw that I figured it out.

"Sweet Jesus. It is to go to the toilet…… it is Brooklax?" I said shocked that I wasn't sick.

Malachy looked at me and I looked at him and the two of us burst out laughing. I had made my first friend in New York.

Maisie-
The Wedding

Thursday morning was like any other day, or at least I thought. I headed downstairs to begin the day. In the kitchen were Malachy and Father John, which wasn't unusual. They were sitting at the table chatting. They were talking about some celebration from what I gathered. I had not told them about the letter from the neighbor at home.

"Maisie, I need you to do me a favor." Father John asked.

"Yes Father, whatever you need." I answered. The priests had been so good to me.

"I know you are scheduled to be off, but I was wondering if you would be able to stand as a witness in a wedding?" Father John appeared to be in a jam.

"Of course, I would be happy to. When is it?" I hoped I had time to find a dress.

"Saturday, I know it's short notice…" Father John's voice trailed off.

"Ok, that's fine. I just might need to pop out to the shop to get something to wear." I said hoping he would offer me to go this afternoon.

"That's fine Maisie, you can have the afternoon off." Father John was delighted.

"I owe you one." Malachy said to Father John.

Malachy looked at me and smiled. I had no idea why. I thought it was a bit odd, but he was a nice man.

I had somewhat of an idea of what I wanted. I ran into Agnes on the avenue. She had told me she was staying in this area with some friends she had made on the ship.

"What are the chances? Where are you off to? Ah, you look excited Maisie." She looked gorgeous today. She had bright blond hair that was pinned up and a burgundy dress.

"I am delighted to see you as well- who is looking pretty great herself." I answered. "I have a wedding; I must stand in as a witness this Saturday. I am going up to Alexanders I think."

"Oh, do you want some company?" She asked.

"Sure, why not?" I answered delighted to see her again.

We got into a taxi at the corner. Agnes chatted about different experiences she had so far and that she had met someone. His name was Charlie. He was American, well Irish American. I wondered if I was going to meet anyone. I know I wasn't outgoing, but still I thought I would meet someone.

"So, you are standing in as a witness? That is nice, just as a favor to the priest?" She asked while browsing through Alexanders.

"Yes, and I think…." I stopped dead in my tracks. It was Malachy, the accountant. It must be his wedding. That is what I was missing.

"Maisie, you were saying…" She was standing right in front of me.

"Oh, nothing." I said. "I mean I think it is for the accountant that I work with."

I realized I was disappointed. Why would I care if he were getting married? That is when I realized it. I liked him. He made me laugh and we often chatted. He was right in front of me, and I didn't even realize it. I took a deep breath and started looking for dresses.

"Come on, tell me. I know there is something you aren't telling me." Agnes had stopped shopping and we started walking toward the coffee shop in the store. She always linked arms with me when she wanted the chat.

We got two cups o' tea and biscuits on a tray. Then we went and sat at a table. It was lovely to do that. It was so nice to catch up. I didn't realize how much I missed her. I also didn't realize how much I missed chatting with me sisters.

"I just, well I guess I thought I would have met someone by now." I didn't know it was true until I said it aloud.

"Maisie, the thing about love is that you find it when you least expect it." Agnes meant well, but I was suddenly sad now.

"I know sure." I agreed.

"Listen Charlie has loads of friends. We are going out to Rockaway next weekend. You can come with us." She finished her biscuit and started to look for money to pay.

"I have this. Let us finish shopping, will we?" I decided to be more positive and move forward.

Myself and Agnes finished shopping and we got loads of beautiful things. We promised to write more and get together.

When the day of the wedding arrived, the weather couldn't have been any better. I changed into a plain navy-blue dress made of a beautiful material with a sash around the waist. I brushed my hair and put gold pins into the side to hold it in place. I chose a light-colored lipstick and some blush. I was never good with makeup.

I was supposed to meet Father John at the back of the church. He said I was to be an official witness for the wedding. The church was cold even though it was the beginning of May. I wished I had remembered to bring my white knit sweater.

There were gorgeous white flowers in the Church. I had never seen a flower like that before. I would have to ask the Fathers what the name of them were later. The stained-glass windows hit my eyes and for a quick few seconds I was blinded. When my eyes came back into focus was when I saw him, Malachy. I knew him, but he looked much different today.

When I saw Malachy, I was sure that it was him that was getting married today. He wore a white rose on his lapel. He looked handsome as ever. I took a deep breath.

Father John came from the side entrance of the church. He was finishing some last-minute bits.

"It's a fine day for a wedding." Father John said, shaking his hand.

"It is." Malachy and I said at the same time.

"Thank you so much for standing in, as a witness. I really appreciate it." Malachy said.

I nodded and said, "Of course."

"Let's get this show on the road." Father John was anxious to start.

Heading to the front of the church, I realized that it was odd that he had not mentioned he was getting married. We had chatted so many times, and it never came up. I had a feeling in the pit of me stomach. I didn't know why.

Malachy walked back up to the altar and his father got up from the first pew and joined him. The doors at the back of the church opened and the music began. A woman, who was much older than Malachy, was wearing an off-white dress with a bouquet of the same flowers that were spread throughout the Church. They were the most beautiful flowers I had ever seen.

From my pew, I watched her smile with a look of happiness I had not seen before. I wanted that happiness. Suddenly, I was overcome with emotion at the beautiful sacrament of marriage.

Malachy's father turned and stepped down in front of the altar. It all became clear; it wasn't Malachy that was getting married. The groom was Malachy's father Hugh.

I wiped a tear from my eye when I saw Malachy looking at me.

I realized so much at this wedding. I realized that there were things that I wanted for myself now. I was here in New York. I had made it through the journey on the boat. I thought about all of them at home. I realized it was okay to be happy and to take a chance.

When it was over, the happy couple walked toward the back of the church. Malachy put his arm out towards me. I placed my arm in his.

"I thought it was you that was getting married." I whispered to him.

"No, not me. Her name is Maude and she is lovely to dad. You also get to meet my brother Hugh. He is going to be a priest." Malachy said nodding over to Hugh.

"You have a lovely family. Well, I had better be off. You have a wonderful day with your family." I said holding back tears. I was missing my family more now looking at all of them.

Mal looked surprised at what I said.

"Maisie, after the ceremony, we are going to the Steakhouse. Will you join us?" Malachy asked.

"Thank you. That would be lovely." I said. I couldn't believe how this day was turning out.

We went to a steakhouse near to the church. It was a quaint little pub and restaurant. The owners were from County Donegal. They had come here a few years before.

Malachy and I talked all day. We had a chance to get to know each other on another level. The owner came out to say congratulations to the happy couple. He moved a few tables, and they found a radio for some dancing. We watched the happy couple dance. They asked us to join them. Malachy put out his hand and we walked to the makeshift dance floor. Moonlight Cocktail by Glenn Miller was their wedding song. While we were dancing Malachy pulled me closer and gripped my hand tighter.

"Malachy, I......" I didn't know what to say. I suddenly felt flustered.

"Don't say a word. You don't have to. I know what you are thinking." Malachy said.

"You do?" I asked, relieved he knew there was something between us.

"Yes, I know you are thinking I am the most handsome man you have ever seen." He said laughing heartily.

"You are an awful devil." I said laughing.

"But can I be your handsome devil?" He asked giving me a spin.

And just like that it was Malachy and me.

Maisie-
Just the Ticket

The Fathers were in the kitchen like every other morning. The doorbell rang and I went to answer it.

"Mary Burke?" A young boy about seventeen said my name like a question.

"Yes, that's myself." I responded.

"Telegram for you." He said handing me an envelope.

I walked back into the kitchen to Father Michael and Father John.

"Maisie, who was that at the..." Father Michael and Father John stood up at the same time.

"It is a telegram. It has to be something bad from home." I put the letter on the table.

"Well let us have a look. Will I open it?" Father John asked.

"The Lord will give you strength." Father Michael said.

It felt like the longest moment of my life. I took a deep breath and felt my stomach get queasy. That was the nerves again when me stomach got like that.

"Your mother is not well. I think you should come home. From, Clare." Father John read the telegram.

Father Michael pulled the chair out.

"Maisie, we are here for you. Whatever you want to do." Father John was lovely.

Going home was not going to be easy. I read the telegram repeatedly. I couldn't even process the words that were in front of me. It was awful. Why did this have to happen?

"Is there anything we can do?" Father Michael asked.

"Well, I was thinking that I might go home to see her." I hoped it wasn't too much to ask.

"For good?" Father John asked with a look of shock on his face.

"God no, I was thinking I would go for a few weeks just in case…." I let my voice trail off.

"Of course. Take whatever time you need. We can sort everything here until you get back." Father Michael said.

"So, you won't replace me then?" I asked, sounding very relieved.

"Don't be silly. Take the rest of the day after lunch and get everything sorted. Sure, we can find someone to just fill in when you are there. We really are sorry and hope everything works out." Father Michael said looking at Father John.

I was so grateful to the Fathers. I was lucky to be in this position. I was looked after and genuinely cared for. It made the transition to New York easy.

"Maisie, Bernadette is a friend of ours from many moons ago. I am going to call down today to see if she can fill in the cooking and the washing while you are gone. She does a few odd shifts here and there. We can tidy the place ourselves in the meantime." Father Michael said it as if he were having doubts about himself.

I hurried up the stairs into my room. Looking around the room, I wondered if I was even going to be able to come back. What if she was too sick? Would Dad expect me to stay? It was all too much to think about right now.

I packed a few of my belongings in my suitcase. After I began to zipper the suitcase, I got an awful feeling in my stomach. The boat. The boat was horrific. It took ages, and the number of times we were sick from a virus and movement. I wouldn't wish that on my worst enemy. It was freezing also. I had never felt cold like that in the West of Ireland. We had felt the chill with the dampness, but never together like that. It was so sad at times and lonely. We knew many didn't make it because it was just too much. They had all sorts of sicknesses, the kinds I didn't even know the names of.

I hurried downstairs to the front corridor. I put on a light sweater as it was still chilly in May. I opened the heavy wooden door and was met with a beautiful sunny day. I thought about the cold, damp day they were having in Ireland. A wave of hope mixed with sadness passed through me that I was going home as I went by Sacred Heart School.

There was no changing my mind at this stage. The only thing weighing on my mind was the boat. This was my only chance to see Mam again with the help of God. I stood in front of the shop that sold the tickets and forced myself to open the door.

A tall man with brown hair and brown eyes walked toward the counter from the back of the shop. He was of Irish descent, but he looked American if that was even possible.

"How can I help you now?" His accent was local, and his eyebrows rose.

"Hello, I am Mary Burke. Most people call me Maisie though. I am looking to purchase a ticket for the boat to Ireland. I need to go home for a few weeks, the mother is sick." I still couldn't believe I was about to get on that boat again.

"Ireland? What would you say if I told you that you didn't have to travel on the boat?" He said with such certainty that there was some other magical way to travel.

"I would say that there must be a mistake." I investigated my purse. I really didn't have time to play games.

"What about an aircraft?" He said.

"Ah, you are joking. That is for the people with money. The ones with the flashy clothes and houses." I was sure he was codding me.

"No, I have been given several tickets for seats on an airplane tomorrow." He held them in his hand.

"Are you serious?" I shouted.

"I just need a few details. I need the passport and a few other documents. You sound like you have not been here too long. When did you come over?" he asked rustling through some papers.

"About two months ago I emigrated. I am from a big town in the West of Ireland in County Galway." I said proudly.

"I have cousins from Galway. God, what is the name of the place? Hang on and I will think of it." He tapped his fingers on the counter as if he were going through a mental list in his head.

"Ballinasloe is where my home is. They have a…" I was cut off and he finished my sentence.

"Horse fair!" he shouted slamming his hand against the counter. "Yes, they have a horse fair there every October. Come from all over Ireland they do." He looked down at the counter proud that he remembered it. There was an air of hope from him that appeared just then and suddenly I wasn't as frightened of the trip.

"Yes, have you been?" I asked.

"No, but I am planning to go over." He said. "Now, where were we?" He put his glasses back on.

"We were working on organizing the ticket. Here is my passport." I held out my Irish Free State passport.

"Ok, Maisie thank you. Let us see what we need to fill out here." I was leaving in the morning. I think that was what he said. And on a plane! An actual aircraft that I would travel on.

I looked around the office. There were stacks of paper on the counter and on several chairs that were meant for clients I believe. The office had long rectangular tables where many papers were spread across. Then from the corner of my eye I saw a small object that looked like a child's toy. Except it wasn't, it was a model of the plane.

He walked around the office in circles at first. He would stop and scratch his head and then walk around again. Finally, he stared at a pile of papers on the chair and picked one up.

He signaled me to follow him. I went into another back office. We sat at a table where I filled out paperwork.

"So, tomorrow morning you will have to get a car out to Idlewild Airport…." He looked over his glasses and paused for me to respond.

"Yes. I will organize that as soon as I leave here." I was relieved that I would not have to go on that boat again.

"Then let's see here about the return ticket." He moved more papers around on the desk.

"Yes. I would like to return in about two weeks if you have a ticket then. And that's the plane?" I asked, praying it was.

"Yes. I will write that up now as well." He left to return to the front of the office where the original papers were.

I organized my money while I had a minute. It was with the money I had been saving to send back at Christmas time.

"Well now Maisie, that seems to be it." He handed me all the papers and then gave me an envelope to place them in.

"I can't thank you enough." I was so appreciative.

"Best of luck to you now." He said.

"Thanks again." I headed out of the shop.

I was flooded with thoughts. What if I needed to go home and take care of mam for a few months? What would I do? One decision and my whole life could change. I was so confused. I didn't even know how I would get to the airport. Would the fathers help me to sort this?

I walked up the avenue and wondered if I left tomorrow, would I return?

Back at the rectory Father Michael and Father John would be back from church working with Malachy and the books. I hoped the fathers wouldn't have told him anything. We had only started to get to know each other. Hopefully, he will understand.

"Maisie, how are things?" Malachy stood up from the office desk. Father Michael and Father John were just finishing their meeting.

"They are okay. Why don't we have some tea? Come into the kitchen." I said, turning away and walking toward the kitchen.

"Right behind you." He said, sounding happy.

I took a loaf of bread out of the bread box. I cut two big slices, one for each of us.

"I think you should sit down. This may take a while." I said praying it would be okay. I turned on the kettle and went to sit down myself.

"Maisie, what is it? If this is not working for you, I understand." He said.

"Oh no, it is nothing like that. My mam is ill. I have to go home."

"And she is back in Galway, right?" He said hesitantly. He took a handkerchief and wiped his head.

"Yes. I am going to go home in two days, but I am coming back. I already purchased the return ticket as well. Also, I will be travelling by plane! Can you believe that?" I tried to sound upbeat as if I didn't know he was worried about me not coming back.

"Well, family is the most important thing after all." He tried to sound positive.

"You believe I am coming back, don't ye?" I asked sitting down in the chair next to him.

"Do you believe that you are?" He asked and I realized how powerful the question was.

"I do actually." I said firmly.

"Then there is nothing to worry about, Maisie." He said as he put his hand over mine.

I felt as if I were floating when he touched my hand. He smiled and he nodded to let me know he felt the same way.

"Are you nervous about the airplane?" He asked.

"I hadn't really thought about it, to be honest." I was lying.

"It will all be fine, Maisie. Before you know it, you will be back making the eggs for the Fathers. You will have plenty to do when you get back as you know those two haven't a clue on how to survive without you." Malachy was laughing aloud.

"All right, I feel better. Thank you, Malachy." I said standing up.

"Well, I will see you to the airport. My brother has the car." He was too good to me.

"That would be lovely. I better start packing." I said, heading for the stairs.

I felt so many emotions as I walked up the stairs. Everything had changed in one day. Suddenly, I was going home, and now the relationship between Mal and myself had become very serious. One thing at a time.

MALACHY-
THE BAKERY ROLLS

When I woke up, I felt differently than I had ever felt. I believed it was love.

And she was leaving. How would I handle this if she didn't come back?

I had never thought of the type to be getting married. I was sure that time had passed for me. I figured that having children wasn't in the cards either. I was okay with all of that. Meeting Maisie had changed everything. Suddenly, everything looked different.

"Someone was back late last night." Hugh said as he burst through the door. He sat on the bed. My brother was a great friend of mine. He always knew when something was going on.

"It wasn't that late." I said fighting back a smile.

"Well, tell me all about it then. I have been waiting to hear what lovely lady kept you out half the night." He said anxiously to hear.

"I don't know what you are on about. I just stopped by the rectory. Father Michael had paperwork for me to catch up on." I tried to hide my worry.

"You aren't getting off that easy. Something's going on, I know you better than anyone Mal. I bet it is about Maisie. You two got on well at Dad's wedding." He was determined.

"I honestly don't know what you are on about." I said as I got up from the bed. I was horrible at lying so I wanted to get moving.

I wanted to tell him all about Maisie. I just wasn't sure of how strong her feelings were. I didn't want to get my hopes up until I saw her again. I hoped she felt the same way as I did. I saw myself walking down the avenue holding hands with her. Maisie would be laughing, and we would be happy together. I was getting ahead of myself; it was only a meal.

But she was going home, and she might not come back.

I had to get my head together. What was I thinking? Did she even want to go out with me again? I was a bit younger too. I didn't know if she realized that.

Hugh paced around the room. I had forgotten he was still in here.

"Well, I will find out sooner or later." He said walking out.

I thought about saying that I left some of the papers at the rectory. I could say I was just double checking the numbers. I would get an awful dose from the fathers if they found out. They would know I was making it up just as an excuse to see her. After my father's wedding and how well we got on, I figured they knew something.

I remembered they had a conference in Manhattan today. Maisie would be there in the rectory on her own.

I would tell her how I felt and that she *had* to come back. I would tell her I loved her.

I quickly got dressed. I decided to stop at the bakery on Woodycrest Avenue and get some fresh rolls. Nino's bakery was on the way to the rectory. Nino's was always crowded. It wasn't just the rolls people went for.

"Ay, Malachy, how are ya? Come and sit down for a minute." He pulled out one of the chairs in the bakery.

"I am well, Nino. How are you?" I figured I had a few minutes.

Nino always had words of wisdom to live by. He always gave advice too. Everyone went to see Nino when they were trying to figure out love, career, or happiness. Nino didn't care about anything except being happy. That is why I ended up there that morning.

"Annie and I we are great. But Momma says she doesn't make the gravy right. I yell at my momma that she is tryin.' What can I do you know? Ya gotta be happy." He said looking to the sky.

"Yes. I was just thinking the same thing. Nino, I met a lovely lady. It is early, but she had changed everything for me." I couldn't believe how easy it was to say it out loud.

"Oh, Mal, that is so beautiful. See, just a few months ago you said you were never getting married. And now here she is." He looked up to motion to God's doing.

"Yes. I guess anything can change at any minute." I said hopefully.

"Life is short. You gotta be happy. I always tell you that. Now, you want some of the rolls to bring to her?" He ran to the back. He came back with hot rolls wrapped in paper.

"Thank you, Nino. I always appreciate your advice." I said taking the rolls,

"I say the same thing over and over again. You gotta be happy. That is it." He said walking back toward the counter.

I took out some change to put on the counter. Nino shook his head. He just smiled and motioned for me to leave. He was very kind.

Walking toward the rectory I felt a nervous, but good, feeling.

When I got to the rectory, I froze. I had no idea what to say when she opened the door. After about a minute or so, I placed my finger on the bell. It sounded so loud. Thoughts raced through my head.

I waited for what seemed like an eternity. The door finally opened. There she was as beautiful as ever.

"Morning Malachy." She said and seemed happy to see me. She stood back gesturing for me to come in.

"Morning Maisie. I brought some fresh rolls from Nino's for us. I actually forgot to get some of my paperwork." I added at the end.

She shut the massive door behind us, and we went into the office. She was super quiet, and I didn't know if that was a good or a bad thing. I didn't know what she was thinking. I automatically went to sit at my desk. She sat in one of the chairs where visitors sat.

"Oh, so you only came in today because of paperwork?" She seemed disappointed. Now, saying that part about the paperwork made her feel badly. I had to fix it.

"Yes, well and to see you." I hoped I had made her feel relief.

"Mal, I wanted to talk to you about last night." She said, taking a deep breath.

She was letting me down easily. This was awful. I felt like my face showed disappointment. I took a deep breath myself. What would I do now? I had to find another job, how could I come here and see her? Was it something I said or did? I raced through last night in my head.

"I understand, you don't want to…." My voice trailed off.

"No, wait a second. That is not what I am going to say. I see the look on your face." She was smiling and she laughed a little.

"Maisie…." How was I going to make this right?

"I wanted to say that I had a lovely time last night." She smiled after she said it. "And I am not just coming back to New York, I want to….well I want to come back to you."

It felt like ten thousand tons had been lifted off my shoulders. I heard it right. I am sure I did hear it.

"I did as well. I am happy to hear that." I didn't know what else to say. Why was I so lost for words?

Now I could tell Hugh the whole story.

"Now, for some breakfast." I held up the bag with the rolls.

"Come into the kitchen and we can have a bit of a chat. I must tell you about my sister Josie. She will be here in a few weeks' time." Maisie said.

"Oh, how lovely." I realized this was important that I would be meeting her family.

"Yes, she is talking about living here full stop." Maisie said excitedly.

"That will be great having your family here. Now, I told you about my brother, Hugh?" I couldn't wait to tell her that he was going to be a priest.

"Yes, you mentioned him. Maybe we could set them up?" She said.

"He's going to be a priest, so that uh…." I answered.

"Definitely won't work then." Maisie said and we both started laughing.

We talked for hours. I looked at the clock and it was half nine. I stood up and walked around the table.

"Now, give us a hug." She said, opening her arms.

I held onto to her tightly. I wanted her to know that it wasn't easy to let go."

"I will come back to you. I promise." She said and she kissed me on the lips.

God, I could never predict what this woman would do next.

Maisie-
Back Across the Pond

The plane itself wasn't too bad. I mean it was shaky and you would be a little nauseous. All that was to be expected. It was an absolute delight compared to the ship. There was a lady she was called a stewardess, that gave you a drink if you wanted it. I don't take a drink. I would just have a bit of brandy on Christmas Eve. I knew too many people at home that would be drinking their heads off, missing work and fighting with their family.

The plane landed in Cork and then I would have to make my way on the train to Galway. It wasn't too bad because I had done it on the way down to the ship. That was when I met Father Nolan. Himself and I became great friends. Malachy also became a friend of his. He was really a lovely man.

When you got off the plane there was a long staircase down to the ground. I felt famous like some movie star, except there was no one there to see me being famous. It would make for a great story though.

I made my way through the airport and got to the train station. I was exhausted from the journey. I was sad as well because my mam was dying.

When I finally got to town, I saw Patrick outside the public house. He was having a cigarette with a beautiful young woman. It made me think of myself and Malachy. She was tall and had dark brown hair-it was almost black. I waved and he looked as if he had seen a ghost. They all knew I was coming home so that was strange. He rushed over to me and your one followed him.

"Maisie, welcome back. God Almighty I am so happy to see ya." He said hugging me.

"It's great to be home." I said. It really was great to be home except for the fact that I was already missing Mal.

"Maisie, this is Kathleen. Kathleen this is my oldest sister, Maisie." He said bursting with happiness.

"Lovely ta meet ya." Kathleen said. I was stunned when I heard the British accent.

"Ah it is." I said smiling. She was beautiful like a supermodel. She was tall like me.

"Mam is taking a turn for the better." Patrick said, taking a deep breath.

"What's that now? Ya mean she is all right?" I was shocked when I heard that.

"Yes, the doctor was there just yesterday. It is why meself and Kathleen are in town." He said with a look of love in his eyes.

"Thanks be to God. I am delighted to hear that." I said relieved.

"Come on, sure we will go back to the house?" He said taking Kathleen's hand and my case.

When we got back to the house, Annie, Kitty and Josie were sitting on the couch having tea and biscuits. They both jumped up when I came through the door.

"Maisie. God, I never thought you would come back here. I figured that I would be over to you." Josie said, taking the suitcase from Patrick.

"Yes, when I heard Mam was ill, I just had to come back." I said, taking off my hat and coat. "I was on the plane and all. It was rough as well but nothing like the boat."

They put the chair in the middle of the floor. It felt like I was on a stage. They began firing questions at me.

"Did you meet anyone? What is the food like? Are you gonna get yourself a house?" They all had questions.

"Where is Mam?" I asked, anxious to see her.

"She is having a little rest for herself. She should be awake in a short while." Kitty said putting her teacup down.

Kitty was quiet. She was always quiet. She lit a long skinny cigarette.

"What are you doing?" I said pointing at the cigarette.

"Oh, everyone is smoking now." Kitty said blowing the smoke into circles.

"I am coming over to you in a few months. I am just organizing a few bits here." Josie said, straightening her skirt.

"Well, I don't have my own apartment yet. I am the housekeeper for the priests. Are you going to stay with Aunt Hanora?" I asked.

"Yes, that will be fine." Josie said.

"Drop her a line anyway and I will tell her when I go back next week." I said.

"Of course." Josie replied.

Mam came out of the bedroom into her bathrobe. She looked very pale, and her hair was not brushed. She didn't look well.

"Mam, God how are you? I am only just back." I said hugging her.

"I am okay now love. I had a touch of pneumonia. The priest was in and all. I couldn't believe it." Mam collapsed into a chair.

"God, I was so scared." I said. I couldn't believe I was home and back with my family. It was like a dream.

"God had other plans I guess." She said almost sounding disappointed.

I sat on the floor beside Mam. I held both of her hands.

"Mam, it will be okay. It is just a matter of getting through the rough time." I realized that her nerves were bothering her. I would always try to be supportive, but she never really talked about how bad it was.

"Did you take the ship?" She asked. She still wasn't looking in me eyes. I turned her face towards me.

"No, Mam I was on a plane. It was amazing. When you are better you will have to come out to see me. Josie will be there by then also." I said looking over at my sisters.

"Yes, we would love to have you." Josie said. Imagine Josie is already inviting her over to New York and she hasn't set foot there yet.

Mam gestured her head back to the bedroom. I stood up to hold her one arm and Annie grabbed the other. We walked her back into the room.

I remember when I was young the doctor came once. He examined Mam and I thought she was going to die.

"It is all in your head." The doctor said one time beside mother's bed. He looked at each one of us with sadness.

Mam would go on. She always did. Sometimes it took longer than usual, but she managed.

It didn't make sense to me either. If it was in my head-then I should be able to rationalize it. However, I couldn't. I never shared my experiences with anyone. Not even a doctor. I would have episodes of panic and insomnia. My stomach would do what felt like cartwheels.

Finally, I talked to one of the priests about it. He said I was probably a bit touched in the head. As long as I went to work and was okay most of the time I wouldn't have to go into the mental. The priest reckoned that I should lay down when I was having an episode. It did help massively.

Mental health is always seen as some sort of neglect on the part of the person suffering from it. They should be stronger or more aware of the feelings. They should do things to distract themselves, so they don't have it.

None of that is helpful. Sure, some of it was okay to try and do. However, there was some sort of guilt and blame surrounding it.

It was awful. It depended on who you spoke to about it. Some people were sympathetic and cared about it. Others would be angry, short, and aggressive.

I knew it was a real thing-that I had to live with. I wondered who else had this other than myself and Mam.

Father Michael-
I knew the whole time

When I found out about the two of them, Mal, and Maisie, well I wasn't too surprised. When you are God's servant here on Earth you can spot true love a mile away. I suspected something right when they were always chatting in the rectory office. Maisie seemed to be making a lot of tea lately, especially when Malachy was working. She made a lovely soda bread as well-, and it was amazing when it was still warm with a bit o'butter. I remember one day so clearly.

I heard a lot of talking and laughing. I thought we had visitors. I went back to the kitchen and saw it was Maisie and Malachy sitting at the table. Malachy stood up and Maisie got up and put plates into the sink.

"Well now, tell us, I am looking for a laugh. What were you two laughing about?" I asked.

They looked at each other and then Maisie looked back at the sink.

"Maisie was just telling me about her brothers and sisters at home. They would be getting up to such shenanigans, especially the night before she got on the boat." Malachy said, smiling.

"Ah, now what do they call it – a wake is it?" I asked. "A wake because you don't know if…."

"You will see them again…." Maisie said the sentence I realized I should not have started. "It is okay Father; it is easier when I talk about it."

I had just been home and some of them said they would come over to me. I know Josie will anyway. She was always looking to go to America.

Maisie took a deep breath as I saw her shoulders fall. She wasn't crying, but there was sadness. Malachy looked at her as if he felt her sadness. No matter what even when Maisie was sad, she stayed quiet. She never complained for a moment in her life.

"Sure, you will see them all again, with the help of God." He said walking over and putting his hand on her shoulder.

"Well Maisie, I am here as well if you ever want to talk." I tried to be supportive. The truth was I was better at listening than giving advice.

"I appreciate that Father Michael, I really do, thank you." She said, taking another deep breath. She dried her hands with the dish towel and attempted to put more water in the kettle.

"Sit down there and we will all have a cup of tea. I can make it Maisie." I said, taking the tea kettle from her.

"No, sure I am alright. I am meant to be making the tea for you." She said laughing.

"Honestly, we can all have a chat there." I said, motioning for her to sit.

The kettle whistled and we all sat. Maisie unwrapped this bread that she had made from scratch. It was a bread that had caraway seeds and raisins in it. I wasn't thinking I would be too keen on it, to be honest. I didn't want to be rude so I said that I would try it.

I took a bite, and it was honestly like nothing I had ever tasted. It was delicious. Maisie said she had a secret recipe for the Irish Soda Bread as she called it. It was a family tradition. She said it was just as good as when she made it at home.

"Maisie, something like this could help you when you get homesick. It can bring back memories and feelings." I said holding up the bread.

"That is true Father, thank you." She said.

Then I saw her look over at Malachy and give him a wink. That was the moment it all became clear to me.

MAISIE-
CHRISTMAS

M alachy had been acting strange the whole week. I didn't know what the story was with him. I was thinking that he wasn't happy. That was silly to think that though, he usually said what was on his mind. He was quiet and not his usual self.

However, I didn't have time to worry about Mal. I had to get the church and the rectory ready for Christmas. It meant I had to get plants and berries to decorate inside and out. Christmas was in three days. I would have to get the linens sorted and create the bulletin for Christmas Day. I was meant to get help from Mrs. McInerney but she had her relatives surprise her for Christmas.

Malachy was in the office in the rectory. He had stacks of paper on the desk in front of him. He looked like he had seen a ghost when he seen me. He took a few papers and covered something else on his desk.

"I am just checking in to see if you were still there." I said looking at the papers on his desk.

"Maisie, sorry I am just trying to get the accounts in order." He said looking back down at his paperwork.

"Oh no bother, do you want a cup of tea?" I asked, hoping he would say yes. Then we could talk, and I could figure out what was going on.

"That would be perfect, but I only have a few minutes." He said standing up but still erasing a figure on a paper in front of him.

He was handsome. He had a smile that looked like he always had something up his sleeve. Mal and I were always laughing. Yes, we had only been together for a few months. As far as his family, I met his father, step-mother, and brother briefly when I stood in at the wedding as a witness. He had met my friend Agnes and I had told him about my family in Ireland.

We sat at the table in the kitchen. I had streams of garland draped across the far end of the table that I was planning to put up in the Church later that day.

Mal sat down and I cleared the area where we would be sitting. He seemed deep in thought. I wanted him to tell me whatever was bothering him.

"Maisie, there is something I want to talk about with you." Malachy said.

"Listen, Mal whatever it is I don't want you worrying about it." I already knew what he was going to say.

"Maisie, let me finish." He said, putting his head down. He knew it wasn't easy for me to allow him to go on, but I obeyed.

"Go on so." I wasn't happy.

"Maisie, I was wondering if you could do me the honor?" He asked, pulling a ring from his chest pocket in his suit jacket. He went to kneel on the floor as well.

"Are you serious?" I asked. I saw the ring shining brightly between his fingers.

"As serious as I ever was." Malachy said, smiling.

"Yes, I will of course." I took the ring and placed it on my finger.

"Let's get married as soon as possible." He sat back in the chair.

"What about…?" I let my voice trail off.

"Your family?" He asked with that smirk on his face.

"Yes, how will they get here for the wedding?" I asked.

"I was thinking about that. I wrote a letter to them, and they just sent something back. It was Annie that responded. She said that they were delighted for us, and we should go home next summer. They will be waiting for us." He said, ending it with a smile.

I couldn't imagine my wedding without my family. I guess traveling across the Atlantic was just too much. I still couldn't believe it. How did he get the address? Ah, he got it from Father John. I had given it to him in case of an emergency.

"Mal, this is....I just don't know what to say." I cannot believe you were writing to them at home." I said holding my chest.

"Maisie, you know I couldn't propose until I knew we had your family's blessing." He said with his shaky voice.

We put the radio on in the kitchen. I didn't think it was loud until Father Michael and Father John came down the stairs.

"Sorry about that." I said bursting with excitement.

"Is there something we should know that happened?" Father Michael elbowed Father John.

"I have asked Maisie to be my wife. Her family gave us a blessing and we are to go over next summer." Malachy said proudly.

"Well- what did she say?" Father John knew well I had said yes.

"I told him I had to think about it. I am only messing." I said laughing. This was all unbelievable.

There was so much to think about. A wedding, a license, and children. Now that was something I never really thought about.

I made us all a cup of tea. We were beside ourselves with happiness. I could barely hold the teacup. We found the most delicious cookies, called Stella D'Oro. They are made at a factory in the Bronx. It is in a lovely area called Kingsbridge. Mal talked about moving up, he told me about a Church there called Visitation Parish.

"Will you get married soon or do you want to wait for the better weather?" Malachy asked.

"I haven't a clue. Maybe soon would be nice." I said with waves of excitement.

"How would you feel about Christmas Eve? Christmas is my favorite holiday. The church is already decorated and all." He said confidently.

I didn't know if I wanted to wait a whole year. That was a long way away.

"That's a far bit way off." I said.

"It is only about two days away." He said, smirking.

He meant Christmas in a few days.

"Yes, I would love that. I thought you meant next year." I said relieved.

Sacred Heart Church was decorated for Christmas, so everything looked so beautiful. I asked the florist to have the same flowers that Maude, Mal's stepmother, had on her special day. Aunt Hanora was a maid of honor. Hugh was the best man. The Fathers did the ceremony themselves. We had a lovely Christmas dinner at Malachy's family in Queens. Malachy's cousins were such good people. We didn't have a lot of people because it was such short notice. Agnes came to the Church as well.

"Maisie, I am so happy for you." Agnes hugged me so tightly.

"Thank you so much for coming I still can't believe I am married." I said looking at the flowers.

"When is the baby due?" She asked touching my stomach.

"What are you on about?" I asked her confused.

"Well over here people get married fast when they are having a baby Just so that everything looks good, I just figured...." Her voice trailed off.

"God Almighty We are not having babies for a while. We fell in love." I said.

"Maisie, I am so embarrassed." She said looking down.

"Don't be worrying Honestly, we are friends for the long haul." I hugged her tightly.

"It is funny though, how could I think that?" Agnes said.

It wasn't the craziest idea to be honest. I suddenly realized maybe I was supposed to be a mother.

Maisie-
The Honeymoon

New York was unbelievably hot in the summer. It felt like 150 degrees. I wasn't used to that kind of heat and humidity. We decided that the summer would be the best time to go over. I had met so many of Mal's family since we were married. I wanted him to be able experience my family as well. I warned him about the boys.

"Tommy, Michael, and Patrick will try to intimidate you. They will make you feel like you aren't good enough for their sister. I am saying sorry now so that you understand and not be worrying about them." I secretly said, praying they would go easy on Mal.

"Maisie, I am well able for them. Don't be worrying about any of it. We will have a great time. It isn't like I can end the marriage anyway. I am stuck with you." He said laughing.

Mal could be very funny and witty. I knew he was only messing with me. It made me feel less stressed.

We arrived in Cork just like the last time I was there. We made our way up to Galway City on the train. Mal had never been to Ireland. His parents were from Tuam but he had never been over. He was mesmerized looking out the window on the train.

"It could be raining one minute and then the next it is a beautiful summer day." He said laughing.

"Yes, that is Ireland. You could have all sorts of weather just in the one day. At least in New York there were the different seasons. One could know how to dress.

"Would you want to live here Maisie?" He asked, reaching for my hand.

"No, I don't think so. It is too hard after you see all the excitement in New York." I was lying. I knew he had no intention of ever moving here. I had to make him think I wouldn't want to move back, or he would feel badly.

The truth was I missed Ireland. I missed my parents and me sisters and even the brothers. New York was amazing. There was no question about how great it was. I just missed them all the time. I felt like everyone was getting closer to one another and myself and Josie were like two random cousins that came back.

They always welcomed me back and we wrote letters to each other, but it just wasn't the same. I was determined to have a great trip no matter what I felt about returning. I could sit around and cry about not living here, or I could have a great time while I am here.

When we got to Carra, me brother Tommy and Kay's house, everyone was there. They had organized a party and made a sign "Congratulations to Mr. And Mrs. Harte." I suddenly flashed back to Mrs. McGovern that had come to the house the night before the wake. She said "M" for Malachy, and she kept saying the word heart appeared. How did she know all that?

Everyone loved Mal which wasn't surprising. They really took a liking to him. We told stories and partied into the early morning.

I didn't want to go back to the States. Mal had been talking about moving to another state. I finished my job in Sacred Heart and he was offered a job in a firm in Philidelphia. I just wanted to freeze this moment. I had my family and I had Mal in Carra. Going back to the States was going to be difficult.

We were packing on the last day of the trip. Mal could see how upset I was. He told me to sit down for a minute so we could chat.

"Maisie, why don't we make a compromise? What if we came back every summer? I am sure your sisters or brothers would let us stay in their houses or move us around. We would only need time off work and the fare for the airplane. I saw how important this was to you. You are so happy here. It is the least I can do." Mal said with a sigh.

Mal was willing to come over every summer. I am sure that there were other places that he wanted to go to. There were places in the United States I am sure that he would want to see. He had mentioned some sort of canyon. We wouldn't be able to afford two trips. He really is amazing.

I really found the most wonderful partner. I was the luckiest woman alive.

Malachy-
The Appointment

It had been going on for a month already. I pleaded with her to see the doctor. She brushed it off as working too hard, the flu and getting older. I knew something was wrong. She wasn't eating, not even the recipe for the Irish Soda Bread that was her favorite. She seemed sad, and I worried about depression.

Maisie's mother was touched by depression. I worried that she was going to get it as bad. Her nerves were bad at times. Other times she was fine.

We went to Union Hospital on 188th Street by the Grand Concourse. She had full bloodwork and a series of tests. They used the words possible tumor and cancer. I kept a brave face.

We would go back a week later when we had results. I had been dreading that day, I was so nervous. I was really worried about Maisie, even though I was the one that insisted she go.

I got dressed quickly and figured Maisie was making breakfast. Breakfast being toast or cereal because she couldn't stomach any meat or eggs. I finished polishing my black shoes and took a deep breath headed for the kitchen.

"Morning." I said sitting down at the table. I smiled in case she was looking at me and felt nervous. I didn't want her to think I was nervous.

"Morning." She answered. "Malachy, you keep looking at me- I am sure it is nothing. Just a virus or something. I have let it go too long."

She looked defeated. They say you know when things are bad. People say they knew they were sick but were afraid to find out. I had to be strong. Even the way she was buttering the bread, it was like she knew her terrible fate was coming.

"Yes, I am sure that is all." I added not looking up from the toast.

"What if it isn't nothing?" She sat down slowly.

"Well, at least we can know and do something about it." I responded unsure if that was the right thing to say.

"Look, we will get through this." I added.

"I guess you are right." She said drinking orange juice. She rubbed her chest with heartburn.

"Listen, I have to get to work at the Church. Father James said I could leave early so I will be in the waiting room when you get out." I gave her a hug and a kiss on the cheek.

Later, I left the rectory. I thought about how this day would change me. Maisie and I were faced with her death or starting over at life. I wanted to travel, and she did also. We could go see her family in Galway. I guess we could either way the diagnosis would go.

I got to the office a few minutes late. The office was immaculate and freshly painted. There were a few women and men sitting at the chairs in the waiting room. I felt my stomach drop. It was all about to be revealed.

A woman in a crisp white uniform was sitting at the front desk. She had bright blue eyes and blond hair that was done in a small bun at the back of her head. She wore a nurse's cap and had a pencil resting on her left ear. On the desk in front of her were file folders that had different names on them.

"Yes, is my wife Maisie here?" I asked nervously. I just wanted to figure it out already. I was sweating badly so I pulled at my collar.

"Yes. The doctor is waiting for you." She smiled.

God, it is worse than we thought. I saw her expression. What was I going to do without her? Was she going to die? My whole body got hot, like I was going to pass out. The nurse led me to the doctor's office in the back. Maisie turned around and she had a look on her face that I had never seen before. Did he tell her or was he waiting for me? The doctor pointed to a chair. I shook my head and waited for him to tell me what was wrong.

"Ok. I think you should have a seat." The doctor put out his hand to offer me a seat.

"Well, Maisie wanted to wait for you. I told her that it isn't what she expected. I assured her that she was not dying." He scratched his head.

I looked over at Maisie and she was smiling. This was insane and no one would say it.

"What is it? Please just tell me." I pleaded nearly bent over in the chair with fear.

"The rabbit died." The doctor shuffled a bunch of papers into a pile.

"This must be a mistake." Maisie went white. The expression on her face suddenly relaxed and turned into a smile.

"I am afraid it is not. The rabbit is 98 percent accurate." He waited for a response.

"What does a rabbit have to do with this?" I was completely lost. This was a quack doctor.

Maisie was smiling and crying. I offered her a tissue from the doctor's desk. I felt foolish that I didn't understand.

"When we do a pregnancy test, Mr. Harte, we take the urine from the woman in question and inject it into a rabbit. If the rabbit dies, the woman is pregnant." He explained.

"It can't be. Maisie has never been pregnant. We have been together for years. All this time I thought we could never have a child......." My voice trailed off.

"It certainly is happening. Maisie is four months pregnant. She should have the baby in late November or December." He added.

Maisie was smiling and fit to burst with excitement. It wasn't that I was unhappy. I was in shock. We never so much as had a question in nine years together about it. Now at 44 years old, Maisie was pregnant.

"Are you happy?" Maisie asked.

"I am delighted, not for the rabbit, of course. But yes, I am going to be a father." I hugged Maisie with relief.

JOSIE-
MAISIE'S APARTMENT

My sister had a beautiful apartment in the Bronx. She loved having people over and especially when I came over with the other sisters. I tried to see her as often as I could. We were close.

One spring morning, I went over with Sr. Anna Therese. Maisie said she wasn't feeling well and could we come over to help little Mary. It wasn't busy on the Monday, so we had no problems.

When we arrived, Maisie was there with the neighbor Millie. She was really a dream to have in the building. Mary and Mal were good friends with them. Maisie would always be baking or cooking for them.

"I am here. I have been trained as a nurse. Let's see what the problem is." I took off my cape and headdress.

"I just want to rest. Josie, I just need someone to watch Mary. Me stomach is sick; I must have a bug." Maisie wasn't warm to the touch.

"When did this come on?" I asked taking her pulse.

"A week ago. I haven't been eating great to be honest." Maisie said. She did look very pale.

"Maisie, lovine, a bug usually lasts a few days at most. Have you any other symptoms?" I was confused at what could be wrong.

"I am only sick in the morning and strong smells. I am sure that having the menstruation as well. It could be that. I am 46 years of age. Some women say that the change is like being pregnant." Maisie sat up suddenly.

We looked at each other. Neither of us said a word.

"You couldn't be Maisie. I mean Mary was a miracle. There just isn't any way you could be pregnant." I dismissed the idea. I was hoping I said the right thing.

"Well, I did have the period a few months ago and then it stopped. I was sure it was the change." Maisie was standing at the window.

"Maisie, now what are you thinking? Is it possible? Have you put on weight?" I asked.

"A few pounds alright and I wasn't eating more." She said suddenly, smiling.

"Is this something you would be happy about?" I asked cautiously.

"Mal and I would be just thrilled." She said hurrying into the living room.

"Sr. Anna Therese, would it be alright if Maisie and I popped into the doctor? Can you stay with little Mary?" I couldn't believe that this was happening.

"Of course, whatever you need. We have cleared the day." Sr. Anna Therese was amazing.

Maisie and I walked down 238th street. There was a doctor just around the corner on Baliey Avenue. Maisie said she had been to him before, and you could just walk in and see if they could see you.

The secretary at the front desk was very nice. She said that he could see us in a few minutes. He was just finishing up with another patient.

We took a seat in the waiting room I thought about how much my sister's life would change. If she were pregnant, her life would be very different. She was 46 years of age. Having a child would be difficult on the body and mind. I prayed to Jesus that He would help her through this.

"Mary Harte, the doctor will see you now." The secretary stood up and called into the waiting room.

Dr. Maloney was a very handsome young man. He wasn't hard to look at. I could still see things like that even though I was a sister.

"Maisie, it is wonderful to see you. I understand you aren't feeling well. How can I help?

"She has been having nausea and missing her period. We would like to have a pregnancy test and see if she is in the "change."

"Josie, I can speak for meself." Maisie snapped and she was usually not like that. "Sorry, I am just very stressed."

"Okay let me examine you and we can go from there." Dr. Maloney took her temperature, blood pressure and pulse.

"No temperature so that is good news. Your pulse is normal, and your blood pressure seems normal as well." He motioned for her to lay back on the examining table.

"Dr. Maloney, we need to find the underlying cause of this. I am a trained nurse as well as being a Sister in the Catholic faith. I would like some blood work done." I was not settling for anything else.

"Yes, I agree. Is there any chance that you are with child?" Dr. Maloney asked.

"I guess anything is possible." Maisie said, scratching her head.

"Maisie, I am delighted. May the Lord bless you in the pregnancy." I was excited and worried. Maisie was 46 years of age.

"I will take some blood and you can come back in a few days. How is Friday?" Dr. Maloney was already headed out of the room. The nurse came in to take the blood.

"Yes, I will bring Malachy as well." Maisie said looking nervously excited.

That next Friday we all returned to the doctor's office.

"Mr. Harte, Sr. Margaret (Josie) I have the results of Maisie's blood-work. I just want to go over a few things before I give you the results." Dr. Maloney was very thorough.

"Is she having a baby or not?" I was wrecked with worry for days. I just wanted to move this along.

"Is it okay?" Dr. Maloney looked at Maisie and Malachy. They both nodded.

"Congratulations. You are going to be having a baby at the end of July or early August." Dr. Maloney was genuinely happy for them, which was beautiful.

"Malachy and Maise, this is a precious gift from our Lord. I couldn't be happier for you." I was beside myself with joy. Mary would be so excited as well. She would be getting a sibling.

"God blessed us with two children, and we didn't even think we could have the one." Maisie said embracing Malachy.

I was so fortunate to have been a part of this day. I could return to the convent and start all the Sisters on the prayers.

MALACHY-
THE ANNIVERSARY

It was our anniversary and I stopped at the butcher and the bakery. I wanted everything to be just perfect. The store windows were all decorated and there was something in the air. It was an air of happiness. I loved Christmas. It was family time and that is why we decided to get married at Christmas 1941.

As I turned the corner, I saw the station wagon. One wheel in the back was on the sidewalk. It was Maisie's sister Josie. No doubt she was here with a load of them from the convent. She always traveled with a pack. So much for a nice quiet evening, I was hoping for hot chocolate and cakes with my girls.

I headed into the building. I stopped at the mailbox. There were a few bills and two letters from her family. I put those into my briefcase. I wasn't going to give them to her until I found out what I was walking into.

It was loud when I got to our floor. I knew there must be quite a few. I put the key into the door and took a guess that there were four nuns counting Josie.

And one, two and three little girls? That didn't add up because when I left this morning, I had two girls.

"Well, hello young ladies." I said, putting out my hand to each one of them. Where did this other child come from? I can only imagine what Josie was up to.

The little girl waved her arms for me to lean down. I leaned down on one knee and she wrapped her arms around my neck. I nearly fell over. She was a girl of about 7 or 8 years old. She had on a bright yellow dress and two yellow bows on her pigtails. She was petite for her age. Her patent leather shoes squeaked loudly.

"Oh, I am so excited Mal." Josie said wiping away tears. "I knew you would just love her."

"What's that Josie? What will I love?" As the words came from my mouth, I prayed they weren't true.

"Happy Anniversary! This is Adele." Josie exclaimed. Behind her I saw Maisie with her head down. This wasn't our first rodeo with Josie. We knew she was capable of something like this.

"Maisie, can I see you in the kitchen?" I politely nodded to the other nuns.

In the kitchen I sat at the table. There were dinner plates from appetizers and half empty glasses with soda. I didn't have the energy to clear the table.

Maisie came into the kitchen. I wasn't upset with her, what could she have done? She looked as if she were about to cry.

"Before you say anything, you know we can't." I stood up and hugged her.

"I know Mal." I knew Maisie's heart broke for the children in the orphanage.

"I just don't want you or the child to get attached. She must go back with her tonight. I can talk to her if you like. We can try to explain it to her." I heard my voice crack.

Maisie sat down at the table. She began scraping the bits of food from each plate onto one plate. Then she stacked the other plates underneath that one.

"Adele's parents died in a car accident." Maisie said, wiping her eyes.

"Maisie I am sure it is awful. We can barely afford the two girls we have." I looked out into the living room. The girls were playing nicely with Adele. It was heartbreaking.

"Everything okay in here?" Josie stuck her head into the kitchen.

"It isn't actually." I started to say when Maisie interrupted me.

"Yes, Josie I don't think we can keep her with us. We just couldn't afford it." Maisie went and took Josie's hand.

"You will have to bring her back to the orphanage tonight. I'm very sorry." I added.

"Malachy, I can't do that. Not tonight anyway. She will have to stay the weekend with you. I signed her out until Monday. You can take the train out to Jersey Monday morning and drop her back." Josie went back into the living room.

I felt Maisie's hand squeeze my shoulder. My face was filled with anger. I know Josie meant well, but it was awful no matter what way you looked at it.

It was just awful.

Then on Monday morning, *before work,* I have to go out to Jersey City on the train. I must bring Adele back to the orphanage, which will not be an easy task. Then I must get back on the train to come all the way back to the Bronx.

Maisie went to the fridge and took out the peaches and cream. She spooned the whipped cream into the crystal filled glasses.

"Mary, Cathy and Adele come into the kitchen." She called. The girls came running into the kitchen one by one. I felt a pain in my heart for this little girl.

The girls carried the peaches and cream out to the sisters. Adele smiled at Maisie and myself.

I told the girls to go to my coat in the hall and see if there was anything in the pockets. I always kept penny sweets in my pocket. Their faces lit up. The least I could do was give her the best weekend I could.

MAISIE-
NOVEMBER OF 1963

I t came out of nowhere.

    Malachy was fine one day and then he wasn't the next.

He wasn't in any pain and that was the most important thing. The doctor said it was a heart attack and it was quick.

But I didn't understand he had only nausea but no real chest or back pain. I didn't know what to do or who to call.

I will never forget that morning.

He died in our bed. He was talking to me. I was holding his head in my hands. I was asking him if he should go to the hospital. He closed his eyes and I looked at the crucifix above our bed. I asked Jesus what I should do.

"Mal, are you okay?" I asked realizing his head had become very heavy.

He must have passed out. He couldn't have just.......I needed to get help. I rested his head on the pillow and told Mary and Cathy to go to the neighbors Millie and Jack.

The girls ran to their apartment as they loved Millie and Jack. I knocked on Cathy Murray's door. She was a nurse. She would know what to do. I told her what happened, and she said that we should get an ambulance.

She rushed past me and into the room. She picked up his wrist and moved her lips as if she were counting. Then she felt his neck. I started to feel very dizzy, so I sat in the chair.

I suddenly realized that she was checking to see if he had a pulse.

She looked down and rested his hand on his stomach. She took a deep breath and shook her head at me.

"What? Why are you shaking your head like that? What is the matter? We have to get an ambulance! Mal, can you hear me?" I ran over and knelt beside the bed.

"Maisie, come and sit down in the chair. I have to talk to you." Cathy's voice was so strange and so formal. It was so unfamiliar to me. Then I heard what sounded like high winds in the bedroom and everything went black.

When I awoke, I was sure that the whole thing was a dream. I looked around and saw the neighbors and Jack standing in the room. I felt the tears leave my eyes.

"Millie is with the girls. Maisie, I am so sorry." I looked over at the bed at Malachy.

"No, please no." I remember feeling like I was having an out of body experience.

I ran over to the bed. I sat on the edge of the bed and laid my head on his chest. I tried to listen to see if I could hear his heartbeat. They were wrong. These things happened where people made mistakes. It had to be a mistake.

I must have been there for a half hour and then a police officer entered the room with a doctor. Cathy, who told me he had passed, was filling out some paperwork in the dining room.

Jack made a cup of tea for me. I couldn't drink it. I just swirled the spoon around in the cup.

"Maisie, you are going to need your strength for the girls." Jack said, taking a deep breath.

"Did you tell them?" I hoped someone did. I didn't want to break their hearts.

"No, but we can be here when you tell them." He said motioning for me to stand up so he could hug me.

The doctor had me sign some forms as well. Then they brought in a stretcher to take him out. I realized that this was the last time I would see him.

"Can I say goodbye before you...." My voice trailed off.

"Yes, of course. We will be in the kitchen." Everyone made their way out of the room.

I sat on the edge of the bed. His shirt was open where they listened to his chest. He had been to the doctor a few months ago. They said he was okay. I didn't understand how this could have happened. He was 53 years old.

"Mal, I don't know how I am going to do this without you. The girls are young, and they will be okay. I am hoping they will be. I am so lucky to have met you. You changed my entire world and how I saw everything. You believed in me and gave me strength when I had none. Please watch over us. I will not ever love anyone else. Please don't let go." I had so much more to say.

I decided that I couldn't tell the girls until my sister Josie arrived. I needed her strength to get through this.

I squeezed his hand and prayed for him to show me he was watching over us.

Everyone was coming back into the room. Father Nolan had arrived and that is when I really broke down.

He helped me stand up and put his arm around me.

"Maisie, you know it is time to go. Let's go and pray." Father Nolan was my rock.

Even though it was time to go, I never really left that room.

Maisie-
A Quiet Sunday

I was tidying up the kitchen after finishing breakfast with the girls. I stood at the kitchen window looking down at 238th Street and Bailey Avenue. We were just back from Mass at Visitation Parish. I was still so sad after Malachy's passing, but my faith helped me get out of bed in the morning. The girls of the St. Anne's Guild were amazing as well.

People were moving about the neighborhood. Some were heading out to a ball game or for a walk in Van Cortlandt Park. Kingsbridge was a lovely area to raise a family. It was close knit. There was a bit of a mix of nationalities as well, but Irish proved to be the most dominant one. Mary Julia and Cathy were in their room playing a board game. They were two very good girls; I couldn't ask for anything else. Just then I heard the tea kettle whistle. I had Josie sneak back a few tea bags from home the last time she was in Kilconnell.

I flashed back to the good times; they were few and far between. It was great to see Tommy, Kitty, Annie, and Madge who came over to Ireland from England. It was great being home that time with Mal. I even thought about moving back home. It was just that the girls were already settled in New York. Josie was also working in Jersey now. I didn't want to leave her.

I poured the boiling hot water into the teacup and grabbed the paper from the counter. On the cover of the Daily News was a photo of a robbery in Manhattan. With my paper and tea, I sat down at the table to relax. I turned the first page of the paper when I heard the tires screech.

I jumped out of my seat and went to the window. Sure enough, it was her and her entourage. The station wagon I'd recognize anywhere. It was a dark burgundy with wood trim. How could this be? She was here last weekend, and I was supposed to have a rest today. Sr. Margaret Burke was the name, also known as my sister Josie.

"Mary Julia and Cathy Pat!" I shouted at the top of my lungs.

"What is it?" The girls came running from their rooms.

"It's Aunt Josie. She is here with a few sisters." I said, twirling around the kitchen unsure of my next move. I stopped and listened to how many doors slammed. Three. It wouldn't be too bad.

"Should we go down to the butcher?" Mary Julia asked, looking for her jacket.

"No, I've a leg of lamb frozen." I pulled it out of the freezer. How would I defrost it? This was a disaster.

"Mom, we can just go down to the butcher." Mary Julia grabbed a piece of paper and sat down to write. "What should we get?

"A few steaks and a couple of bags of spuds should be enough." I thanked the girls and gave them some money.

"Ok Mom, we will be really quick." Cathy's voice trailed off.

I took the leg of lamb and started hitting it against the corner of the counter. My friend Mary Carey told me it might work if you are in a jam. When I saw that it wasn't working too well, I was glad that I had sent the girls down. I put it in the fridge to defrost it later in the week. I put a few vegetables in a dish and an onion dip that a woman at the church showed me how to make in a jiffy. I heard the buzzer and it made me jump. I pressed the buzzer for the lobby. I hurried into the living room to fluff the pillows and fold the blanket. The apartment looked presentable.

This was quite typical of my sister. She would arrive unannounced all the time. Much like any nun, she always had a few of the sisters with her. You just wish that you would know these things ahead of time.

Suddenly, the door flung open and through it came my sister Josie and the other sisters. The girls must have left the door ajar.

"Isn't this beautiful?" She exclaimed, walking into the apartment.

"Hello Josie." I said, turning off the television.

The other sisters waited by the door for me to motion for them to come in. They were all quite reserved compared to Josie.

"Isn't this wonderful, Sister Margaret?" One sister asked. Whenever they entered the room, they would announce and ask how wonderful or amazing everything would be. No matter what the room looked like, it could be a disaster area, they would say everything was great.

"Yes, this is a surprise." I answered, trying not to sound sarcastic.

"See, I know you love surprises." She said. She began the process of removing her habit.

After the sisters finished removing their cloth, I gestured for them to sit on the couch. Sister Assumpta was a wonderful lady who also came from the West of Ireland in County Clare. She was a tall, strikingly beautiful sister with an even more beautiful heart. She longed for home, so she returned often to see her brothers and sisters.

"Now Sister Assumpta, will you be going home for the summer?" Josie even asked the question as if she already knew her response.

"Yes, I'm going back for a fortnight. It will be short and sweet." She smoothed her skirt and reached for a small plate. She put two slices of vegetable and a tiny smear of onion dip on her plate. The sisters never overdid anything except praise for the Lord. Honestly, one sister told me that one time. They also took only what they needed in many aspects of their lives.

Sister Magdalene was much more petite than Sister Assumpta. You often had to ask Sr. Magdalene to repeat her responses or to speak up. Her heart was massive, she was a very generous and thoughtful woman. Her focus and devotion were to help the poor and unfortunates. The two sisters sat properly on the couch and waited for Josie to address them rather than initiate the conversation.

Josie was always the center of attention. Everyone always knew that Josie had arrived. She would make a grand entrance. She was natural at being fearless and a powerful leader. I never knew growing up that Josie had the calling. She experienced it much later in her life. We always knew that Josie loved children, so we all assumed she would be married with a family. We were shocked when we found out she was entering the convent.

Thinking back, I will never forget that day. It was a sweltering day in September when she told myself and Malachy that she was joining the convent. We were out in Rockaway at the beach. It was like being on a vacation far away and you could still go home that night. We were at the Bungalows. They were my favorite spot on 54th Street. I knew some of my friends from home went there. We were having a glass of lemonade and the hot sun was blazing on my face when she said it.

"Maisie, I have something to tell you." Josie was beaming with excitement.

"You're getting married?" I jumped up from the chair. I knew the engagement would be short because they had been together for so long.

"Well, not exactly. I'm not marrying Jack." She said nervously.

"What does that mean?" I was completely confused now.

"I am going to get married to Jesus." She said holding on to the "S" at the end.

"Who is that? You met someone named Jesus?" I knew she went on vacation recently, but she had not mentioned anyone. I was quite sure that was a Spanish name.

"Jesus. I mean the son of God." She looked down as if she were hoping for me to be okay with it. I felt like I had entered some type of alter universe.

I repeated the statements in my head over again. She meant she was going into the convent. She was becoming a nun.

I realized I had been standing in the middle of the living room in a daze. I quickly sat down bringing my attention back to the sisters.

"Where are the girls?" Josie asked as if I were hiding them from her.

"They have just gone down to the shop." I said, wondering what was taking so long.

"Oh, I hope you haven't gone to too much trouble for us." Sister Assumpta looked worried.

"No trouble at all. I just forgot a few bits and sent the girls down to get them at the butcher." I stood up to go look from the window when I heard their patent leather shoes in the stairwell. They burst through the door making it slam against the hall closet. They had two heavy shopping bags.

"Oh, hello girls, how are things?" Josie and the other sisters stood up.

"We are fine." Mary Julia said. They carried the shopping bags to the kitchen table. Returning to the living room, the girls took their coats off and hung them on the door to the closet.

"Well, come here and tell me all about school then." Sr. Assumpta said.

I picked up the bags from the table and hurried into the kitchen. I wanted to get the potatoes started so I could see how the leg of lamb was doing. I had a feeling the steaks were going to come in handy.

Mary Julia came into the kitchen. She didn't want to be in the living room I was assuming. The sisters could be a little too inquisitive and pushy about calling. Mary Julia was a very curious, bright girl. She had a drive to learn things and wanted to be with adults more than kids. If she were with children, she would be the one pretending that she is the mommy. I didn't think she would have a calling.

"What do you need help with mommy?" She asked folding the brown paper bags.

"Can you get the sisters a drink?" I asked stirring the mix for the sauce.

"Sure." Mary Julia said. She carefully took three Waterford Crystal tumblers from the cabinet. We used the crystal on holidays or special occasions but especially when the sisters came. She poured a little more than a shot into each glass. The drink had to be Harvey's Bristol Crème. Josie would not drink anything else. I followed Mary Julia into the living room with the bottle, I knew the routine.

"Mary Julia let's have a look, hold up the glass." Josie always inspected to see if the glass was clean.

"Here, Aunt Josie." Mary said holding it up.

"Beautiful. Thank you." Josie said, taking the glass

I held the bottle in my forearm with the label facing her. She had to be presented with the bottle before you poured it, she always thought someone was trying to give her the "cheap" stuff as she would say.

"Maisie, come sit with us." Josie moved over to the sofa.

"I will of course." I said placing the glasses down on our coffee table.

"The girls told me they are doing well at school." Josie was proud of them.

"They are doing great actually. I was only just at the teacher conference. Math and science are a bit challenging, but they are starting to get it. School today is different from when we went in Ireland." I said with a sigh of relief.

"That's wonderful ladies!" Sister Assumpta was a teacher. "Would you ever be a teacher?"

"Uh, I am not sure. I want to be a nurse in a hospital with lots of people I can help." Mary Julia never told me that she wanted to be a nurse.

"Mary, I am surprised. I didn't know you were thinking about nursing." I wondered if she didn't want me to worry about money for college. Now that I thought about it, she would make a wonderful nurse.

"Yes. The other day we were researching different jobs at school. That one seemed really exciting to me." She said, taking a sip of her soda.

I went into the kitchen to check on the steaks. I had no idea how I would pay for nursing school. There were loans I was sure, but would I be eligible? If anything, it was only a small thing to worry about.

"We are having steaks and potatoes in a bit. They are almost ready." I shouted from the kitchen.

"Thank you so much Maisie. You are too good." I heard Josie yell from the living room.

I heard bits and pieces of the conversation from the kitchen. They were chatting about the summer and what the girls were doing. Our sister Kathleen, we called her Kitty, was supposed to come for a few weeks and stay with us.

I returned to the living room just in time. We had a few minutes before the dinner was ready. Josie took a deep breath and said, "Mary Julia, do you ever get the feeling that you want to devote your life to Jesus?"

Mary Julia spun her head around so fast to look at me. She didn't know how to answer at all. No matter what the response it would never be the right one when it came to Josie.

"It's a big decision. I would want to be sure." She took a deep breath while answering. I was proud because that was the most sensible and thoughtful response.

"Cathy and Mary go on and wash your hands before dinner." They jumped up as if they had won the lotto.

I wish I had the strength Josie had. She wasn't married. She didn't have a husband to take care of her. She didn't act lost without one either. She was helping others, which was amazing to me.

It was a lightbulb that went off at that moment. An epiphany came over me. She did have something that kept her strong. Devoting her life to Jesus was what made her strong. She looked to give her heart to Jesus in helping others. Her faith drove her, and God kept her strong.

I was lost. I was devastated. I had lost Mal. He was my rock. I knew he was always with me, but I wanted him here beside me. When he passed, I felt like I had lost everything. I realized I had to change my perspective. I had been lucky enough to meet my soulmate and the love of my life. Some people never have that chance. Josie's visit was a sign. It was God calling me back to my faith. I had been to church many times, but I wasn't *there*. I needed to put my heart back into my life.

"Well sisters, it is time for dinner." I put down my sherry.

"You really shouldn't have gone to all this trouble Maisie." Josie said.

"Thank you so much for coming to see me today. I know you care so very much." I said holding back tears.

"Of course, Mary God knows when we need something." She said nodding her head.

"In the Name of the…." Josie began.

"Please allow me to say the prayers today." I said knowing she was pleased at my effort.

So much for having a quiet Sunday, but this was exactly what I needed. I looked over at Mary Julia just in time for her to wink at me.

Uncle Jimmy
aka Monsignor Nolan

"Come on Rambler." In the rectory vestibule, I felt a cold burst of air as I opened the door. It was a beautiful Christmas morning indeed. North Broadway was so quiet at this time of the morning. Rambler was my alarm clock. Sometimes it was five or five thirty in the morning. He would put his wet nose on my forehead to get me up and moving. He is a great friend and a gentle giant.

We walked up to Untermeyer Park like we did most mornings. The view of the Palisades was breathtaking. I often thought it would make a wonderful location for filming. I threw the tennis ball to Rambler. He ran out far into the distance. He came running back proudly with the ball in his mouth. I looked at my watch. It was a few minutes to six thirty. Mass was at seven sharp and I had to be there a few minutes early to set it all up. Annie would have started breakfast and I wanted to get back. I whistled and Rambler came back from one of the beautiful flowers.

I thought about how lucky I was today and every day. I think about it often. I had always wanted to be a priest. I remember being a little boy at Mass, and just knowing that would be my job when I grew up. My grandmother and uncles always talked about a "calling." I wasn't aware that this was a feeling that overcame someone. I literally thought it meant that the priests "called" around to everyone's house and asked, "Do you have anyone here that wants to be a priest?" It is funny if you think about it. It was Father

James that helped me when I was younger. He was the one who was there for me when things got tough. He was a kind and patient man and that is the type of man I wanted to be.

This morning the Masses were beautiful, Annie had the Church decorated with massive poinsettias. Everyone was dressed up and the Church was full of life. I have to say though I had a very good attendance every week at Christ The King. My homily was filled with life lessons and ideals my church community could relate to. After the Masses, I went to the Ford Fairlane with Rambler. We were heading down to Maisie's for dinner. Maisie and I met many moons ago on the ship when she first came over.

Lately, I spent a great deal of time with Maisie. I was trying to help her with her faith. It was understandable because she lost her husband so suddenly.

I got to Maisie's about one in the afternoon. Rambler ran right in jumping on the furniture and the girls were screaming.

"Well girls, how are we today?" I burst through Mary's door like I did every time.

"Uncle Jimmy!" The girls were all excited.

I took off my long coat and hung it on the coat stand. They looked at each other. I know they asked me to bring candy, but I didn't like them expecting it. When they saw that I didn't give them anything they then resumed playing with the dog.

I had some candy in my pockets for the girls as they loved a surprise. It was a penny candy. Maisie's girls asked me if they could get the gold coin chocolate. They saw some commercials on the television while they were watching Bonanza. Cathy was always looking for Satellite Wafers, which were the newest craze.

I went into Maisie in the kitchen. I would give them the sweets later.

"Maisie, how are things?" I said entering the kitchen.

When Maisie was quiet, it made me worry. There was a different expression on her face. I felt I wanted to help her feel better. Some people yell and some people don't get out of the bed when someone dies. Not Maisie. She went about the day and was quiet.

"Oh, you know as best as can be expected." She said as she was cutting a turnip. She was peeling it over the sink and seemed to look millions of miles away.

"How are you doing? Are you going to the counselor at Visitation?" I hated bringing it up, but I figured that I would say it early and then not be worrying about it all day.

"Yes, and it has been helpful. It has helped me cope." She said.

"The firsts of everything are always the hardest. Especially the anniversary of his death." I said pulling out a chair for her to sit down and talk to me.

Being a priest wasn't about saying Mass but taking care of people. Maisie was a good friend of mine. I wanted to be here for her as a sort of vehicle to God, to bridge her to opening to God again. I knew she never gave up on the Church, God, and her faith, but she lost her husband. She was left in the country with very little family and two young little girls. She was angry, frightened, and confused. She had many questions that she had no answers to.

"Yes, these holidays are very difficult." She took the dish towel and wiped it in a circular motion on the table.

"It won't get easier, but you will find peace and a new normal." I knew that was a hard realization to come to.

"I suppose." She said. "I just don't know what to say. I worry when I talk about him to the girls. I mean they understand he is gone, but I still miss him too. There just wasn't enough time. I can't understand it. He didn't have pain. He was only sick to his stomach that day."

"That is why I recommend the counseling. There are many women there who are going through the same thing." I was going to leave it at that.

"Yes, I know. I will be going next week." She added. "We just had so many plans. We were all going to go to Ireland next year. All of that is gone now. I feel so hopeless Father."

Maisie took a deep breath in and held it. I watched her chin shake as she tried to hold back the tears. I stood up and went over to her.

"You can call me Jimmy if you like. I told you that loads of times. We met before I even said the final vows." She laughed because she couldn't imagine herself calling me Jimmy.

"Mary and Cathy, come on in and help me set the table." I called out to the living room.

"Josie and her entourage will be here shortly. I must get the turkey out, and let it cool a bit. I want to put the stuffing into a bowl." Maisie said looking overwhelmed.

"Well, if you give me something to do, I can help. I have to admit, I am not great at all these things." I said and she gave me a look.

"Now, you know the kitchen isn't your place. Will you go in and see what these are up to?" Maisie was determined to get me out of the kitchen. Maisie would do a great job collecting herself and moving forward. I just worried that she was pushing her grief further away and not dealing with it.

The girls were playing with Rambler in the living room. The television was going in and out. I adjusted the antenna, but it didn't seem to make a difference. I decided I would give the girls their candy-no I had better wait for it after dinner. Just then the buzzer went off, and Mary ran to the wall to push the button to open the door downstairs. It was probably Josie.

Cathy and Mary ran to the door to open it for their Aunt and the other sisters. Sister Margaret, Maisie's sister, entered in her full dress along with the other sisters. Josie, as everyone called her, was a ticket. She was a ticket, meaning she was quick with her wit and wasn't afraid to stand up for herself. She is a woman ahead of her time.

The Sisters settled in, and Maisie put out a small bar with a few selections of whiskey and scotch. Josie had the other sisters get her drink and mine as well, which wasn't necessary.

"Uncle Jimmy," she called me that even when she wasn't in front of the girls, "tell me how the Masses were this morning?" She didn't wait for a response and went back into the kitchen.

All the nuns turned around simultaneously as if they had the winning Bingo number. Josie nodded as if she had given them a signal to pay attention.

"They were wonderful, I have to say. The church looked beautiful and there were so many in attendance. Thanks be to God." I always had to feel like I had to be "on" when Josie was here.

"We had a lovely few Masses this morning as well. Reverend Laurence Cardelichio came over from Our Lady of Sorrows and said a beautiful homily." Sr. Assumpta said smiling.

It was then I heard a tremendous thud in the kitchen. Maisie stuck her head out and gave me a look to get into the kitchen immediately.

"If you will excuse me, Sisters." I said as I headed back into the kitchen.

That was when I saw it. Tom, our dinner, was on the floor. Rambler looked at me with the saddest eyes.

"Help me get it back on the plate. Rambler, I tell ya I am not in the mood for this today." Maisie said as she started to laugh.

We lifted the bird back onto the plate.

"The signs are everywhere." I told her to look up.

"How is your dog knocking the turkey off the table a sign?" She said puzzled.

"You laughed." I said pausing. "Mal sent you a sign. It is not a vision, or a thing. You have to be open to it. You have to believe Maisie."

"Ah, stop. Malachy did love the pranks. Are you serious?" She asked with her eyes filling with tears.

"I am serious. Malachy is always with you. Open your heart, your eyes, your mind, and your ears. He is everywhere."

I felt so thankful that Mal sent her a sign.

Maisie-
The First Trip back to the
Old Country

I couldn't push it off again. I had already put off the trip so many times. Reading Annie's last letter broke my heart. They were so worried about me. I was managing as much as I could. I guess they just wanted to actually see me. It would be great for the girls as well. They could meet their cousins. Josie would be on the flight too. Her shenanigans always proved to make things better.

We hired a car to get to Idlewild Airport or Kennedy Airport, whatever they are calling it now. I remember he was shot a few weeks after my Mal died. Even though Jackie Kennedy was a First Lady, she was a widow like me. Suddenly, she would have to figure out a new life without her husband. It was challenging.

Mary and Cathy tried to hide their excitement. Josie was going as well. She could always help you in her own way. I knew they were all excited. It was hard to feel comfort, excitement, happiness, or any emotion for that matter. I almost felt like I didn't deserve it. Mal wasn't here so that meant nothing would be good again. I knew that wasn't what he wanted, but that is what we were working on in counseling.

During counseling, Mrs. Walsh would sit across from me in the office rectory side room. There was no table so she would fold her hands on her lap and turn her head from side to side. Her hair was always tied into a perfect twist.

"Do you think, Maisie, that Mal wants you not going to your St. Anne's Guild Meetings? What about just going to the park with your children?" Mrs. Walsh asked as she straightened her skirt.

"No, I know well he doesn't want me moping around the place." I answered simply. I knew he would not want me to be sad for the rest of my life. I just felt so guilty if I was happy about anything.

"No one is saying that you are going to be happy the way that you were with him. But you could try and find a new normal." She knew what she was talking about. She was a counselor or something like that.

Which is why I decided it wouldn't be any harm to go home.

The plane took ages. Sorry, let me correct that. The plane was amazing. It was nothing like that horrible boat I had taken on the way here the first time.

It was dawn when we got to Shannon. It was a beautiful airport. My brothers Tommy and Michael came to collect us.

"Well, I never thought I would see the day." Michael hugged me tightly and I felt relieved.

"God, it is good to be home." I said. "These two lovely ladies are Mary and Cathy. And you all know Josie of course."

"Uncle Michael and Uncle Patrick!" The two girls jumped up and down.

I had not seen them that happy in ages. They weren't happy for ages I guessed. This turned out to be a good idea. I couldn't wait to get back to Carra.

Everyone was at Carra. They were all waiting for us. It was so exciting and overwhelming at the same time. I felt guilty, but I had to push through for the girls. I also knew Mal would want me to enjoy myself.

We opened the door and were greeted by so many. All of our siblings were there. Michael, Patrick, Tommy, Kitty, Annie, Josie, and myself. God there were so many of us.

Everyone was eating and talking. It couldn't have been any better, I thought. I felt a chill down my spine. It was an old Irish superstition that when you get a chill, it means a loved one was with you. I thought about Mal at that moment. It was like Father Jimmy said, you just have to be open to the signs. They are there.

"Maisie, we have a welcome home cake for you and the girls." Kitty said, placing it on the table.

I went to grab a few forks from the drawer, but I must have opened the wrong one. It was a drawer filled with notes, pens, matches, and scissors. I went to close the drawer and it was stuck like it wouldn't shut properly.

I pulled the drawer all the way out. An old envelope fell to the floor. I picked it up and looked inside.

It was filled with stamps. I looked at the handwriting and realized it was Mal's writing. The last time we were here he had brought part of his collection. He was so proud of it. He wanted to have a stamp from each country in the world. When we arrived back in New York after our first trip he realized that one of the envelopes was missing. I told him that he left it at his cousin's house in Tuam.

Somone shoved it in the drawer and forgot about it.

Except Mal didn't forget about it. He wanted me to know he was there with us.

I finally felt some peace.

KITTY-
THE FIRE BRIGADE

Mom, Maisie, Kitty, Josie, and I were just sitting down in the sitting room after the dinner. It was lovely having all the sisters over together. It was already so dark at half-four in the afternoon. The winter was so unforgiving. It seemed like summer was so long ago. The laughs from the summer were all gone.

I turned on the kettle to make the dessert for the tea. Looking out the kitchen window, I saw Mattie herding the sheep. With Dad being gone, Mattie had to take over. We all helped as much as we could. It was all a great deal of work, but soon Mattie would be married. As the eldest son, he inherited the land and the house. He had already insisted that we had plenty of time to organize things. He said we could stay too if we liked. Mam would have her own room, of course.

To be honest, I was excited. Myself and Nancy were thinking about finding somewhere ourselves. Women were not supposed to be leaving the house before being married. Husbands were not supposed to die so young either, changing the whole plan for the family. Mam was brave through it all. Poor Maisie had lost her husband as well. It was just awful

Tonight, I was meant to go to the céilí with Nancy, but it was much too cold of a night. We agreed that we would leave it until a fortnight. We usually went to the Aughrim Parish Hall dances or the ones in Ballinasloe.

"Mam, do you want any sugar in the tea?" I called from the kitchen.

"Just the drop of milk, love." Mam answered.

Nancy and I have our tea the same way, with just milk. The sisters all settled into the sitting room for the night. I found a book that I was hoping to finish. It was so cute having all the sisters in the house.

I woke up suddenly coughing. The smoke had not filled the house so I realized it must have been outside. I ran to see if it was something in the kitchen, when I saw through the window that the fire was out in the barn.

All of us were heading out the kitchen door and hurried away from the barn. Mattie got all the animals out of the barn just in time. Nancy then went to the neighbors to call the fire brigade. When we realized that the fire was contained in the barn, I brought Mam and her sisters back into the house. I waited at the window inside for the fire brigade to come. When they arrived, I joined Mattie outside to speak to the firemen.

A tall firefighter walked over to me and asked, "Is everyone accounted for, and okay?"

"Yes, we are all okay. Thanks be to God." I said, noticing how attractive he was.

"Who is the owner of this land?" He asked, looking directly at me.

"My brother, Mattie is the owner. My mam, sister and I live here with him." I answered.

"What do you think started the fire?" He was waving to the others to pull the house out towards the barn.

"I don't know, it happened so suddenly." I said.

"It could have been a cigarette. You would not believe the damage a cigarette can cause." He said straightening out the hose.

"The animals are all accounted for as well." I added.

"Right now, I will do my best with the guys here. I will talk to you inside before we leave." He said winking his left eye.

I did see that wink. Was he flirting with me? At a fire? No, I must be imagining it. I went back inside to sit and have a cup of tea. I had no idea what we were going to do. We had no money to rebuild the barn. I didn't want to ask Mattie, as he was exhausted. After some time, the firefighter I had been talking to prior came into the house. He tipped his helmet and took it off, placing it on the chair by the door.

"Do you mind if I come in?" He asked. I noticed how handsome he was in the light of the kitchen. He had dark red hair and sky-blue eyes.

"Of course." Mam ushered for him to come into the kitchen.

"I am with the Ballinasloe Fire Brigade. My name is Patrick Cahill. Most people call me Pat. It's nice to meet you, just sorry about the circumstances." He said, standing in the middle of the kitchen.

Nancy shoved me in the side, I jumped. Nancy knew well, I thought he was handsome. She just knew things; I don't know how. I didn't want to be embarrassed, at least not in front of him.

"This is my sister Nancy, my mam, I am Kathleen. But everyone calls me Kitty." I said. Why did I say that? Now it was awkward.

"Nice to meet all of you." He smiled and looked around the kitchen.

"Why don't you come in and sit down for a minute?" I said trying to compose myself. "I'll make a cup of tea."

"That would be nice, as long as I am not putting you out." He said sitting at the table in the kitchen.

Nancy rolled her eyes and walked out of the kitchen. Mam took her tea into the living room and winked. She never missed anything. Mattie headed outside to inspect the damage.

"Kitty why don't you sit down yourself?" He asked, pulling out the chair beside him.

Honestly, as if I would sit beside him and not across from him.

"How do you take the tea?" I asked.

"Just milk, I am sweet enough." He said smiling.

I tried not to laugh out loud. There was something about him. He had confidence and a presence. He wasn't like anyone I had ever met before.

I brought the teas over with a few biscuits. I took a seat across from him. I stirred my tea and waited for him to say something.

"Do you ever go to the Aughrim Parish Hall dances?" He asked choosing a biscuit.

"My sister, Nancy, and I were thinking of going tonight, but we decided to stay here." I couldn't believe it.

"I was actually going to go tonight as well. Isn't that funny now? We might have met up there." He gave me that head nod and a wink again. I quickly looked down. He was so forward.

"Yes. That is funny." I answered.

"Well, I might be going to the next one in two weeks. Do you think you might go?" He asked.

"Probably, I might see you there then." I stood up to put my cup in the sink. I was so nervous, and I had no idea why. I didn't know if Nancy and I were going, but all of sudden I wanted to.

We chatted and asked about people we knew. Suddenly, he stood up.

"It is getting late, I just realized. Thank you very much for the tea and the company." He said smiling after.

"Thank you for putting out the fire. I don't know what we would have done without you and the brigade." I couldn't tell if that sounded genuine or not.

"Well, see can you get those animals sorted for the night anyway." He put on the helmet and walked out the door.

"It was nice meeting you." I called out.

"I'll see you at the céilí. We can chat more then." He then walked off. I had a feeling that it wasn't the last time I would see him. At least, I hoped it wouldn't be the last time.

MARY JULIA-
THANKSGIVING

We were at my mother's apartment, the same apartment I grew up in, West 238th Street and Bailey Avenue. It had not changed much over the years. I was hoping after Christmas I could get Mom to move in with us or with my sister, Cathy. Thanksgiving was Mom's favorite holiday. I think it was on the menu. She said a Thanksgiving meal was as close to being in Ireland as you could get. Of course, they didn't have Thanksgiving in Ireland. However, the food we ate on Thanksgiving was very similar to things she ate when she went home to Ireland. Mom was an expert; she had celebrated the holiday since she arrived in New York almost sixty years ago.

I had stayed over to help her get things sorted. She was running around the small kitchen all morning. I was trying to help, but it was hard to help as she wanted to have everything just right. "Let's get Tom into the oven." She yelled from the kitchen. She needed help lifting him.

Mom wasn't dressed, but she had her floral pastel colored housedress with the snaps. I loved those dresses. She had them in so many colors and designs. She motioned for me to walk around her and get started on the sweet potatoes.

"You get started peeling those potatoes." I took them off the counter and pulled the garbage from the corner of the kitchen. Then I could easily shave the skin pieces right into the bin.

Sweet potatoes are very hard to peel and cut. They are all different sizes and shapes. They could be shaped strangely, and the skin could be tough. Everyone was always worrying about cutting themselves. But I very rarely ever did cut myself.

We had about people coming. Mom, my sister Cathy and her husband John, Frank, Monsignor Jimmy Nolan, Aunt Josie and Frank's family coming for the dinner.

We made a list of all the things we needed to do in the next few hours. Vegetables, bread, pumpkin pie, and stuffing still all had to be done. We had plenty of time and had an hour or so before we had to do anything.

"Mom, you want to watch the parade?" I turned on the television and sat on the couch.

"Sure. I remember the first time I saw the parade. I was with my Aunt Honora when I was working in Manhattan. She told me that we would have time to have a quick look at the parade before I had to be back." She said stopping in her tracks.

"Come and sit for a minute then." I moved over a bit to make room.

My mom sat beside me and wiped her hands with a towel she had been using in the kitchen. Her eyes were glued to the television now. I felt a sudden wave of nausea, which was very unusual for me. It was just my nerves. I also was a bit dizzy on and off the last few days.

It was probably nothing. I can't imagine it would be…. no. Wait, am I pregnant? I turned to tell my mother and realized I had to figure out if I was even late. I got my work schedule out from the hospital out of my purse. I counted, and I was two weeks late. How did this happen? How did I not notice this?

The doorbell rang. It was Frank's parents, Katherine and Frank Senior. They were a little early, but it was no problem.

"Hello everyone." Frank Senior was so friendly. He was a New York City firefighter in the Bronx. He could definitely tell a great story about his experiences. The fireman were the real heroes.

"Hi Mom and Dad. How are you?" It was difficult to call him Dad because my father had passed. It was important to Frank that I call him Dad. I was getting used to it.

"The parade is great, look at how excited the kids are with the balloons." Mom looked at me as if she knew.

"Yes, adorable." I said. I decided it was too early to say anything. Mothers knew though, they were able to pick up on those things.

I just had to get through the day and take the test when I got home. I didn't even think about how he was going to react. I am sure he will be happy. We always said we wanted kids, so it may have just happened. Again, I had to wait for the test results. I had taken a test from the hospital just in case.

"I'm going to get started on the vegetables. I told Josie to be here at two o'clock. We can get them ready and then get them in as they arrive. You know how she is." Mom said standing up.

At 1:25 in the afternoon, Josie and the sisters arrived. Josie arrived as if she were royalty. She expected everyone to get up when she arrived. Someone should take her coat, fix her a drink, and immediately entertain her. You put up with her antics because deep down she was lovely and would do anything for you.

"Well, welcome to my sister's lovely abode." She said handing me her cape and headdress. All the sisters were behind her, Sister Assumpta, Sister Mary, Sister Bridget, Sister Anne, and Sister Francine. The sisters nodded at me very shyly and sweetly.

"Come in everyone. Have a seat and we will sort some drinks." My mom said.

I took all of their coats and put them into the bedroom. We would lay the coats on the bed because the closet didn't have enough room.

Heading back into the living room, the nausea hit me again. This was going to be harder than I thought. The sisters were sitting in the living room when I got myself together. Mom must have poured their drinks with Josie's help. I was looking for a ginger ale.

"Mary Julia, come and sit down next to me. Any grandchildren for my sister? You know you don't want to wait too long. You might miss your chance." She said everything that she was thinking.

"When the time is right, Aunt Josie." I said.

"Well, you look very healthy, at least since the last time I saw you." She was saying that I put on weight. Healthy meant I was eating, and it was noticeable. It wasn't a complete insult, but close enough.

"Mary Julia, tell the sisters what is on the menu for the dinner." She picked up her Harvey's Bristol Crème and made an attempt at an air toast to the group.

"Turkey, mashed potato, string beans, turnips, rolls, and sweet potatoes are on the menu. There are also a few other things, that were just off the top of my head." I said, realizing I was not hungry at all.

"Sister Assumpta, is that okay for you?" Josie asked. It wasn't like if she said no that didn't work for her that we would start cooking something else. What did she expect?

"Everything is just grand. Thank you so much for having us. We were just at the orphanage with the children. God love them." She said, taking a deep breath.

"We don't realize how fortunate we all are." Josie shook her finger in the air.

She was right, we didn't realize how fortunate we were. We get caught up in day-to-day life and forget all the things God has blessed us with.

The buzzer rang. It was Frank and my sister. They all took a ride over together.

"I'll buzz them in." I said getting up. There was dizziness again.

I just realized that I had not eaten anything all day. That was all it was. I sometimes get heartburn or dizziness if I don't eat anything. I didn't know if I was trying to convince myself.

The apartment door stuck. It was even more involved to open because she had the police lock on the door. You had to slide the bar and open the door at the same time, which was no easy task. Mom had it down to a science, I never quite mastered it.

"Hi guys! Happy Thanksgiving!" I managed to greet them before I had to sit down again.

"Mary, how are ya?" My sister Cathy asked.

"I am ok. I am coming down with something." I started backing away, so we didn't embrace.

"Yeah, you might be coming down with a baby." She whispered quietly leaning in so only I heard her.

"Don't be silly." I quickly responded. The look of panic came over my face. I couldn't hide it.

I quickly pulled her away so no one else could hear us.

"Oh, my goodness…." She covered her hand over her mouth. Her eyes widened like saucers.

"I didn't take the test yet. So, I am not sure, but I am definitely late." It was a relief to tell her.

"Oh, that would be so lovely, I am so excited." In her eyes I could see she was already dreaming of unicorns and rainbows.

"Let us just wait and see. I have the test in my purse, and I will call you tonight after I take it." I wanted to move on for now. It was just too hot, and I was feeling overwhelmed.

"Does Frank know?" She asked.

"There isn't anything to know yet." I walked back into the apartment.

We all said hello to each other. I didn't want to make a whole thing of it. Even if I was pregnant, it was too early. I went into the kitchen to help Mom.

"You can start the string beans." She was working hard here.

"Hi Mom." Cathy kissed our mom hello.

"Cathy, how are things? How was work last night? I hope you got some sleep." Mom was always so worried about her.

"Mom, I am fine. Let me help." She spoke.

"Ok, get started on the salad." Mom said.

We went to the dining room table to work on the salad. I knew she was going to start talking about it, but Frank and John were standing having a beer. We began setting the table and putting the food out.

"Let's go to the bathroom now and take it." She whispered with a mischievous look on her face.

"No, not now." I said. "What if someone needs to use the restroom?"

"Honestly, sometimes you are just so…." her voice trailed off. "You go in and take it, then close it up again and we can go in the bedroom to look at. It takes a few minutes, doesn't it?"

"Oh, I didn't think of that." I was really starting to get nervous.

"Mary, do you want something to drink? I got that wine you like." Frank said across the room.

"No thanks. Not yet." I realized this had to be done now.

I nodded at Cathy, and she went to the bedroom to wait for me.

I got the test out of my purse and headed to the bathroom. I took the test and closed the plastic cover on it. This was it.

I went back to the bedroom where Cathy was waiting. She was pacing back and forth. You would think this was her taking the test.

"It should take five minutes. That is what it says on the wrapper." This was going to be the longest five minutes of my life.

"How many minutes left?" Cathy asked now, sitting in a chair at the edge of her seat.

"Four." I said softly.

Just then Mom came in and went to her dresser. She saw the test. "You know how I found out that I was pregnant with you Mary?"

"Mom, I don't even know yet." I said almost upset I didn't tell her.

"It is fine. I am glad you shared with your sister." She said.

"How?" I asked.

"How what?" She asked.

"How did you find out you were pregnant with me?" I asked.

"Well, I actually thought I was dying. I was 44 years old, tired and sick all the time. Then they took a urine sample, and I came back a week later. They injected the urine into the rabbit and if the rabbit died-you were pregnant." She said still in disbelief.

"So that's how you found out? The rabbit died?" Cathy asked.

"Yes, we were in shock. But we were so happy." She said, smiling.

"Time is up." I said.

"I will let you be." Mom started to walk out of the room.

"Mom, are you kidding? You can't leave now." I took her hand and sat her on the bed.

"It's two lines. You are going to be a grandma, and you will be Aunt Cathy and I will be Mom." I said not believing it.

"I have so much to be thankful for this year. Let's tell everyone." Mom was so excited.

"Can I tell Frank first?" I called him into the room.

"Ok, we will leave you to it." Mom and Cathy left the room.

"What is it, Mary?" He looked at me and I realized I still had the test in my hand. "What is that?"

"Congratulations. You are going to be a dad." I said.

"Wait, you can tell from that thing in your hand?" He was shocked and sat slowly onto the bed.

"Yes, we are going to have a baby." I liked the sound of this.

"I still can't believe it." Frank was happy, but in shock.

"Well, if it is a girl, I get to name her, and a boy you get to name him." I suggested.

"Sounds good to me. Frank Jr." He said.

"God, I hope it is a girl." We both laughed out loud.

We went back out to the living room, and everyone sat down except me. I gave a look to Frank to get up and fortunately he understood that he should stand next to me.

'We have something to tell everyone." I said looking around the room.

"It is about time. We were wondering if it was ever going to happen." Aunt Josie said excitedly.

"Yes, it finally has." I said.

Aunt Josie never held back, but we loved her for it.

MAISIE- THE CRAYONS

Three grandchildren didn't seem like a lot, until you were watching them at the same time. I remember the first and only time it happened.

Mary told me they were going to dinner for their anniversary. So, then I would have little Catherine to mind. I could stay at Mary's that night and be back at my daughter Cathy's house the next morning. They only lived down the hill.

Cathy was great to open her house up for me to live in when I was deciding what my next move was. Cathy was my youngest and she was married to a man named John. They had a little boy called John Malachy and Julia Helen. Cathy was easy-going and it was nice to stay there. I liked going back and forth between both of my daughters' houses.

"We are all set for Saturday night then?" Cathy asked as she was folding the laundry. I was assuming she meant she knew I was going to watch Catherine my granddaughter.

"Yes, I am staying with them overnight. It is easier and then I will be back on Sunday morning." I said looking back at the television. It was Three's Company that was on, one of my favorite shows.

"No, you are watching Johnny. I told you we have those concert tickets a long time ago." She looked frustrated.

"Oh, that is fine. I can watch them all here. It is not like they are babies." I don't know if I was trying to convince her or myself.

"Yes, as long as that is okay for you. Yeah, you should be fine." Cathy sounded confident. "I'll call Mary now and let her know."

* * *

Saturday night I made a huge pot of macaroni and cheese and a tray of chicken nuggets. You couldn't go wrong with macaroni and cheese; all kids love that. Cathy and John were tidying the house.

"They are only going to make a mess of it." I said hoping they would just finish getting ready.

"Okay Mom." She shouted.

After a while they came downstairs, dressed, and ready to go out.

"Are you sure you are okay?" Cathy was worried. She was folding towels and leaning on the dining room table. She looked as if she were going to say that they weren't going.

"It will be grand. I promise." I was almost positive that all would be fine.

Just then the doorbell rang. It was Mary and little Catherine. They came in and Mary and Cathy went upstairs.

They could be as thick as thieves or acting like they didn't know each other. They were probably up there trying to figure out how one of them could just stay home. I swear to God they are the worst. You would think that I had never seen a child before.

After a while they came downstairs.

"Look, one of us can stay. We are not saying that you cannot handle it, but it is a lot." Mary said looking concerned.

"Honest to God, will you go?" I said, passing them in the kitchen. They looked at each other and shrugged their shoulders and headed for the door.

They already knew not to say goodbye to the children. I told them they will only set them off. I told them to slip out.

"Ok guys, time to eat." I yelled. I headed into the kitchen and began bringing the food to the dining room table.

Each of them had their own specific favorite bowls. Catherine had a strawberry shortcake bowl, Johnny had G.I. Joe bowl, and Julia had a My Little Pony bowl. Then, I realized I had forgotten to get them drinks.

"Hot, hot, hot." The kids were yelling. God almighty this was going to be a lot of work. I hurried to get the drinks. John came into the kitchen to help.

"I'll help Grandma." He yelled.

"Just a sec, Johnny, I think the top is loose…" I yelled. As soon as the word came from my mouth, I felt the cold Hawaiian Punch spill down my leg.

"Oh, I'm sorry Grandma…." Johnny said.

"It's okay. Go back to the table and I will sort this out." I grabbed a roll of paper towels. After cleaning it all up, I headed back to the table. This was not going to be easy.

For a few minutes they were calm and eating. I quickly thought of something for them to do next. A movie would be great. We can turn some lights off and we can try to calm down.

"Okay everyone, let us head into the living room. It's movie time." I said with enthusiasm.

"Yeah!" The two of them were shouting and jumping. They jumped on the couch, and I sat in the chair.

"Now, who knows how to work this VCR?" I was so confused. There were so many buttons. I still had a black and white television with the knobs on it. Now, there is so much more technology, and it is changing every day.

"I can help." Cathy was always trying to be responsible and helpful.

I just sat in the chair and waited. Kids were better at figuring out this stuff. Then I remembered I had been doing laundry. I went to the back kitchen to get the clothes from the dryer.

Some toys were scattered on the floor with a coloring book and crayons. I was lucky not to break my back. I opened the dryer and folded the clothes. I transferred the freshly washed clothes into the dryer when I heard a crash.

"What was that?" I yelled.

"Nothing." The two yelled back.

"Whatever you do Grandma, don't come back to the living room." Johnny said.

I hurried out. They had broken the beautiful vase from Waterford in Ireland. It was such a beautiful crystal vase. It had beautiful cuts in the crystal that made the light sparkle so much during the day. It was lovely by the window.

I cleaned up the mess and put shoes on us so that we couldn't step in broken glass. I hurried back into the laundry room and put on the dryer. I could still have the clothes done before they got back. I went back to the living room afraid something else had gone wrong.

"Grandma, we put on Ghostbusters. Come sit in the middle of us." Johnny motioned for Cathy to move to the right or left. I watched for about an hour and did a decade of the rosary in my head. They were so into the movie they didn't see me get up to go fold the laundry.

I opened the dryer and saw a white washcloth with some blue all over it. I couldn't imagine what that would be from. As I pulled more of the whites out, I began to see a rainbow of colors. It was almost crusted into the fabric. Then on the floor I saw it, the empty crayon box with a few loose crayons. I realized that one of them must have tossed the crayons in with the wet clothes. All the whites were stained. John's work shirts, Julie's white dress and Cathy's nursing uniform were all ruined.

I put them all in again with bleach knowing that there wasn't a chance, but I wanted to be hopeful.

Defeated, I went back to the living room. They were so cute; it was hard to stay mad at them.

"Right, it's almost time for bed. Let us get the living room all cleaned up. It's like a hurricane came through." I waited with my hands on my hips.

Johnny went to the kitchen and wiped down the dining room table and Cathy fixed the cushions on the couch. This was easier than I thought.

I got them up the stairs and into pajamas. Mary and Frank would pick up Cathy already in her pajamas.

"Grandma, thank you for being so nice to us. Mommy would have been yelling at us. She never would have let us watch that movie either. I love you." Cathy said.

"Thanks Grandma." Johnny gave me a strong hug.

"That's what grandmas are for." I said to her. I was sure there was no harm done.

I went back downstairs and sat down with the Daily News. I survived. The house survived too. I saw the car headlights come through the dining room window. I heard the key in the back door.

"You have them upstairs and in bed already? Wow, great job! Did they give you a hard time, Mom?" Cathy was taking off her coat.

"They were no trouble at all." I spoke.

"Oh, thank goodness, I was worried. I thought it might be too much for you." She said laughing.

"I would order a few more uniforms because a couple of socks got into the whites. I ran it through again." I was praying she wasn't going to look now.

"And you did laundry?" She was shocked. Then she said, "John and I might go out more often."

"Oh, and one more thing, about that Waterford vase…." I let my voice trail off.

"It's fine, Mom." She said heading up the stairs.

I didn't do too bad, not that I wanted to be doing this every weekend. I decided that next weekend I would take that bus from 231st in the Bronx all the way down to Atlantic City.

CATHERINE-
THE MIRROR

It was summer. August was particularly hot this year. Records were broken and they never stopped talking about it on the television. My mom had said that she would buy me an air conditioner in the fall when the sales were on. I would have it for next year then.

My mom was putting my laundry away in my drawers. She wasn't quiet because she was slamming the drawers. It was a passive aggressive way to get me up.

"Cathy- it is time to get up. We have to go to Kennedy." She said sitting down on my bed.

"Is that today?" I asked with desperation.

"Yes. Let's get moving. I don't want to hit traffic." My mother said leaving the room.

We arrived at the airport on time. Their plane was supposed to arrive at three in the afternoon. I couldn't believe how many people were at the airport. Many had signs that had a huge apple for New York or a person's last name held up by a man in a suit.

The airport was hot because of the heat and the amount of people moving around. It was filled with smells of coffee and different aromas.

We stood behind the metal barrier and waited. We saw quite a few people smiling pulling their bags with a string. There was one man that had a shirt on that read, 'I kissed the Blarney Stone.' He was with a woman and two children also wearing tourist type shirts.

It was then I saw my grandmother's face. She wasn't smiling. She had on a navy suit, her white pocketbook and a small suitcase. Aunt Josie had her head down as well.

My mom signaled for them to move to the left when exiting past the barriers. My mom rushed through people to get to her.

"What happened Mom?" My mother asked, grabbing the bags.

"Tommy died. He was buried yesterday." She said wiping a tear with a napkin She took a deep breath.

"Why didn't you call me?" My mom was almost yelling at my grandmother.

"Now what difference would that make?" She said almost yelling back as well.

"I could have talked to you or sent money." My mom was hugging Aunt Josie now as well.

"The Lord has his ways, dear." Aunt Josie always had a sentence like that ready.

We began walking back to the car. Aunt Josie had me pull her suitcase. She put her arm around me. No one was saying anything. I didn't know who Tommy was or what happened.

"Sometimes the Lord calls for us, Cathy." She said with a set of rosary beads twisted through her fingers.

"Ok Aunt Josie." I answered. I thought this was going to be exciting It wasn't.

We got to the car and my mom loaded the suitcases into the trunk. Even though I complained about going to the airport I actually loved picking my grandmother and Aunt Josie up after a trip. Now there was no smile or happiness.

"He must have had a stroke." Aunt Josie finally said what happened.

I didn't know what a stroke was, I thought it had something to do with the heart. What was surgery then? How come some people could go to the hospital and be okay?

"Was he in the hospital?" My mother asked.

"No, it all happened at home. We are still in shock." My grandmother said Her face looked really tight like she was angry.

"I'll tell you now darling-when they put me in the ground the sun will be shining. I promise you that." Aunt Josie looking up towards God.

"And it will pour from the heavens on the day they put me six feet under. It will be like everyone is crying." My grandmother said.

"Please stop talking like that. I am trying to drive." My mother pleaded with them.

The two of them were always talking about what would happen when they died.

My mother was upset. She was worried that my grandmother would feel pain. My mom didn't want anyone to feel pain. When someone had pain, my mother would get angry.

Aunt Josie opened her pocketbook. I had never actually seen the inside of hers. My grandmother and Aunt Josie had the same pocketbook. You never knew what was in the bag, but there were always surprises in it.

She took a very large bar of Cadbury's chocolate out of the pock-etbook. From what I could see there was also a napkin, a roll and a small liquor bottle. I was thrilled. I was just getting the gold wrapper off when I heard my mother.

"I hear that wrapper back there Catherine. Remember you still have to have dinner." My mom said looking at me through the rearview mirror.

I sat back. I broke off a rectangular piece from the bar and handed it to my Aunt again. I mouthed the words 'Thank you.'

While I was eating the chocolate, I happened to look at the side mirror of the car through the window. I saw my grandmother and the sorrow all over her face. I saw her wipe one tear with a rolled-up tissue she always had stuck in her watch. I broke off a small piece of chocolate and passed it to her.

"Here Grandma, some chocolate will make you feel better." I said really hoping that I helped her.

"Ah, thank you Cathy. It already has." She said, breathing heavily.

EILEEN-
FRED'S

Every summer we went to the Catskills. We went in a whole group together. The girls, Union crew, we had a lot of different names that we call ourselves. It was Cathy (Mary's sister), Mary, Susan, and me. We stayed in this one spot every year. They were efficiencies, but more of a hotel. We also brought our mom's if we could. Maisie always came. She would help out with the kids if we wanted to go out at night. She was good like that.

We used to get a block of rooms and we would go back and forth to each other's rooms. We would entertain my son Sean, Cathy's Johnnie and Julie, Mary's daughter Catherine and Susan's two boys. We definitely brought the energy wherever we went.

We would have a BBQ or hang out on the grounds of the hotel.

One particular year something happened that none of us will forget.

We were at Fred's Motel. It was the last few days of our trip. We had already hit all the spots- Howe's Caverns, the Mystery Spot, the German Festival and Carson City. On this particular day we went to the pool.

It was a beautiful day outside. It was hot-but not too hot that you couldn't enjoy it. Susan and I were at the pool with all the kids. Mary and Cathy went to the office at the motel to see if there were any events on that we could go to that night.

I was reading a book. It was a Jackie Collins novel, but it was too bright to be reading. The glare was too much and then I would have a headache. I decided I would finish it later on. I counted the children like I always did. It didn't matter where we were whether it was an amusement park or the backyard, I always counted.

Except this time, I was off. There was one missing. I knew that none of them went with Cathy or Mary. I scanned the pool area and the fence and beyond. My eyes went back to the pool area. Out of the corner of my eye, I saw a shadow in the pool. I immediately jumped into the pool and grabbed Christopher. I had no idea how long he had been in the pool. He wasn't wearing his arm swim bands.

I laid him on the side of the pool. He wasn't conscious. I had to put on my nursing armor and not my Aunt Eileen armor. I had to have a clear and unemotional head.

I checked his mouth and realized I had to begin CPR. Thankfully, he started coughing before I even got into the process. He coughed up a lot of water. I heard a piercing sound behind me. I realized that had to be Susan screaming.

"He is okay. He is breathing." I said. The adrenaline was pumping through me. I felt as if I were going to pass out.

What if I had not seen him? What if I ran out to the road instead of looking at the pool? Thousands of thoughts flooded my brain. I was happy that I was already on the ground, I probably would have passed out myself.

"What happened?" Mary and Cathy were running toward the pool.

"He almost drowned." I said, realizing my voice was shaking.

"Thank God you were here." Cathy said, turning her head towards me.

I was so thankful that he was okay. What if I did try to save him and he didn't make it? Why were all these scenarios running through my head?

I will never forget that day. Ever. It was one of those moments that made you really realize that it could be all over in a second. A family wouldn't have their child's first day of school or Christmas morning watching them open presents. One second can change anything.

JOSIE-
GORT

"**D**id you pack everything?" Maisie asked me at Mary's house.

"Everything, but the sink it looks like." I said.

Maisie and I decided we would go back home to Gort. Gort itself wasn't our original home, but we have been going for so long it feels like it.

"Mary has the tickets." Maisie said as she was cleaning out her purse. It was her classic white pocketbook. Last week I saw her take out a roll, wrapped in a napkin, and a packet of jam on it with a plastic white knife. She had everything in there.

"Ok, let me know what I owe you and I will give you the money." I said, placing my hand on her arm.

Frank, Mary Julia's husband, had just picked me up from the Villa Marie Clare. Mary insisted that I was ready ages before we had to leave. Frank was coming in and out of the house with coolers, plastic bags and suitcases. Frank was a quiet and kind man. He could be quite funny as well.

Frank knew about my faith. We were passing a cemetery one time.

"When they lower me in the ground for my final resting place on Earth before I go upstairs-the sun will shine brighter than anything you have ever seen." I said.

"Well, I know the heavens will pour tears the day I am lowered." Maisie said laughing.

We had no fear of death We were leaving here to move on to Eternal Life.

"Aunt Josie, are you sure you aren't going to get charged for any of this? These cases weigh a ton." He looked at Mary and she shrugged her shoulders.

"Dear, I won't be charged anything extra and Maisie is travelling with me." I am a Sister of Charity We have certain perks.

"Mom, here is your boarding ticket. I put it inside your passport." Mary said, handing it to her. She did the same for me.

"Mary Julia, will you come home again soon?" I asked my niece.

"Not this year, but I am going to take the girls soon. Maybe next Easter." She said handing us each sandwich. "You better it this, you know how the airplane food is."

"Ah, thank you Mary. You are too good to us." Maisie said.

"Yes. We would never be able to sort out any of this." I added.

Frank came in again and asked if we were ready to hit the road. We gathered our small bags and headed out the door. Mary was coming for the ride as well.

We got on Cross County to the Hutchinson River Parkway heading to John F. Kennedy Airport. Myself and Mary Julia were in the back and Maisie was up front with Frank. The traffic was bad enough so there was time to chat.

"You won't come back to the old country Frank?" I would ask him every time I had a chance. I knew the answer was always going to be the same.

"No. Josie. We had a great time, but I saw everything I needed to see. If I do decide to go, you will be the first to know." He said laughing.

Frank turned on the radio to 101.1 CBS FM radio. We all liked the oldies but goodies. "Run around Sue" by Dion DiMucci was playing on the station. We all sang a few different words. Frank told us that when that song came out it was 1961 and he had just turned 21. It was also around the time he had his '54 Corvette. Whenever this car was brought up, you saw a wave of nostalgia. He still has the car in a garage in Riverdale. He has been working on it. I have never actually seen it. But from what I heard; it was quite a vehicle. It was white with a maroon interior. The car was a classic.

We got to the airport after quite some time. We parked the car and went into the gate. Mary and Frank held the suitcases, and we got our passports.

The girl at the Aer Lingus desk was wearing a kelly green skirt suit. She spoke with an accent and was from County Cork.

"Now ladies, you will be travelling from JFK to Shannon. Is that correct?" She said with a smile.

"Yes. That is correct." I said.

"Now I have to ask a few questions. Did you both pack your own bags and know the contents of your bags?" She paused.

"Yes." We both said simultaneously.

"Are you carrying any lighters, matches, fireworks, food of any kind in your suitcases? This is forbidden by all airlines." She said looking up from papers she was stamping.

"Well, I am not sure that you realize I am a Sister. I shouldn't have to answer questions." I was annoyed.

"No, there is nothing in their cases. I checked myself." Mary said.

"Now, we have seats, together, don't we?" Mary Julia asked, leaning on the counter.

"Yes. They are in the aisle and a window. Two seats together." She smiled.

"Ok. Great. Mom, we are going to start heading back. We don't want to hit too much traffic." Mary Julia leaned into Mary and hugged her for a good minute.

Then she hugged me and whispered, "You take care of her for me?"

"Of course." I whispered back and moved toward a hug from Frank.

"Thank you so much for driving us. We really appreciate it. We will ring you when we get back." I said.

"Josie, will you come on? I want to get something to eat before we get on the plane. I am starving and you know how I feel about the plane food." Maisie said already headed past the shamrock banner toward the gate.

"I am right behind you." I said, waving at Mary and Frank. It was a pity they weren't coming with us.

We found McDonalds at the airport food court. Maisie loved McDonalds. She usually has tea and a hamburger. She usually ordered the Happy Meal and then gave the toy to one of the grandchildren.

Maisie and I ordered our food and went and had a seat. The food court area was filled with many people. She always said she could spot which ones would be on our plane.

"See your man over there in the stripe top? He is definitely on our flight." She said pointing over to his table.

We would try to see if we could guess who would be on our flight.

"Ok, I will pick out the next one." I looked around our section and found a young lady with jet black hair and green eyes. She was wearing sweatpants and a grey hooded sweatshirt with sneakers. "Her." I said proudly.

"Yes. Good one." She said. "I am really looking forward to going home. Who knows how many times we will be able to go?"

"Speak for yourself Maisie." I said slightly irritated with her. We were in our seventies. It wasn't like we were that old. We had our wits about us.

"I guess you are right." She said. "At least three or more times I would like to go back to Ireland."

I stirred my coffee and watched the coffee swirl. I suddenly realized how I didn't feel my age. It frightened me. I wasn't afraid of death I just wasn't ready to go.

Margaret-
The Passport

Frank came to get me because the car service was meeting us at Mary's house in Yonkers. He was very good to me. I didn't drive and I lived right by the hospital, everything I needed was right near me. Sure, the neighborhood wasn't what it was, but it was fine for me.

"Hey Margaret, let me just pull in and I will get your luggage." He backed into a spot and got out of his white Plymouth Reliant. "This is some crew you got going with you today?" He was always so friendly and making jokes.

"Yes. Frank, you should have come with us." I said to him. He went once when he and Mary were married in the 70s. He never went back. He just said he didn't like the plane.

"I know, but somebody has to work and pay for this." He laughed.

"I hear you." I got into the car while he put my suitcases in the trunk.

We drove and chatted all about the Bronx and where he worked. Frank was a technician for NYNEX, New York Telephone and AT&T. He had some interesting experiences working. The Bronx itself was interesting on any given day.

When we got back to Mary's he said, "Now keep an eye on them. They get all flustered and they put down their pocketbooks and the money is falling out. You know how it is."

"I will of course." I said.

Mary and Frank's house was a gorgeous English Tudor in Yonkers. It had great character; it was truly an amazing house.

"Well hello Cathy." I said entering the vestibule.

"Aunt Margaret!" Cathy ran from the stairs to greet me. I was Cathy's godmother, which truly meant a lot to me that Mary asked me. I hugged her tightly.

"Are you all ready for this trip? We are going to have so much fun. I can't wait for us to all meet up in Dublin."

"Yes, I can't wait." Cathy said.

"Madge, how are you?" Josie, Maisie's sister, got up from the chair to say hello.

"I am fine Aunt Josie. How are you?" She was all set for the trip as well. She was in full dress.

"Isn't it a beautiful day? I can't wait to get to the old country." She always sounded as if she was being facetious, but once you knew her you realized she wasn't. She could have been an actor if she wasn't a sister.

"Yes. Maisie, how are you?" I went over to Maisie signaling her not to get up.

"What can we do with her?" Maisie whispered in my ear about Josie.

"We have to keep her at this stage." I whispered back.

I sat down on the couch. Everyone was here. Mary was upstairs finishing up odds and ends. She had her hands full, two little girls and her mother and her aunt.

"Margaret, come up. I am just finishing up a few things." Mary yelled from the stairs.

"Coming." I went up the stairs.

"Josie already greeted me with her usual sunshine." Mary said, putting on her earrings. Mary was slim and tall with dark hair. She kept brushing the same piece of hair so it would flip just the right way. She did this when she was nervous.

"What could Josie have said to you already?" I laughed.

"Well, I came down the stairs and she didn't even say hello. The first words out of her mouth were 'If you think that looks good on you, then that is all that matters.' I was beside myself. I could see if I had asked her how I look." She looked through her jewelry box and I sat in the chair.

"She is unbelievable you know that." I was trying to be supportive. Josie could be critical, but it wasn't in a mean way. She was honest and sometimes it hurt. One thing you knew is that she would never lie to you. When she said that someone looked great-she REALLY meant it.

"I know. I just want everything to go right." She said, turning around to give me a hug. "Sorry, she has me in a spiral."

"Try to remember, Pat is picking you up and the O'Donnell's are getting them. You only have to survive the flight." I said positively. "John is driving you and me. That is Patrick's nephew. He is such a nice guy. The only thing he has a fast car. Phil also said he has a nickname, "The Fugitive." It will be interesting.

"This is true." She said. Mary wanted everything to go right. With Josie anything that could go wrong would.

We went back downstairs, and Josie was going through the tickets and passports.

"Mary Julia, I don't see my passport." She said as if Mary was being scolded.

"That is because you were supposed to bring it with you." Mary said.

"Don't you, have it?" Josie was searching for her black patent leather pocketbook.

Just then Frank, Maisie, Cathy and myself simultaneously headed over to Josie's chair and asked, "What?"

She didn't have her passport. She left it in Saddle River in New Jersey. It was about forty minutes from here. We had to get on the road to John F. Kennedy Airport to check in for the flight. Forty minutes there and forty minutes back. We didn't have that kind of time.

"What do you mean? Do you not have the passport with you, Aunt Josie?" Mary spoke slowly as if she were talking someone down off a ledge.

"I thought you had it. Didn't I give it to you at Easter?" She was still searching through her bag.

"Josie, how do you not have it?" Frank was getting frustrated. He headed for the door and walked outside.

"Let me check again." Mary was getting flustered. Stuff was spilling out of the bag, Irish money and snacks.

"Here, let me help." I took Josie's bag and placed it on the coffee table. I honestly had no idea what we were going to do.

"Josie, did you put it in your suitcase?" I asked, walking over and pointing to what I thought was her suitcase.

We would never make the flight if we had to go back. I was praying and searching through her suitcase. It was filled with sheets, towels, and food. If anyone opened it, it would be confiscated.

Frank was talking to Mary in the kitchen about a plan. I packed every-thing back up into the suitcase. They could tell from my lack of shouting that I had not found it.

"Oh, here it is. Call off the dogs." Aunt Josie held it up waving it like a flag at the Olympics.

Mary came running out of the kitchen, "Where was it?"

"Dear, you are going to get your blood pressure up. It was beside me next to where I was sitting. It must have fallen out of my bag. That was bet-ter that this happened here and not the airport." She was proud of herself.

"Yes, it was." Mary was relieved.

The doorbell rang. Frank went to answer it. It was the car service to pick us up.

"Wait until you see this guy." Frank came back laughing.

"Of all the gin mills…" Mary said picking up the suitcases.

"At least we have the passport…" I added.

Mary laughed and said, "Come on, let's get this show on the road."

MARY-
THE PICKUP

Picking up Maisie and Josie from John F. Kennedy Airport was no small task. You never really knew what you could be faced with. The best thing they ever brought back from Ireland was my cousin Gerry. I am not kidding. They brought him back to spend the summer with my sister Cathy and me. This was just the type of thing that they did.'

The two of them kept it interesting. All the brothers and sisters kept things interesting. Josie, Annie, and Maisie were a match though. They were all the best of friends that fought like cats and dogs. Josie always made an entrance wherever she went. Maisie and Annie were always laughing about something they noticed or sometimes nothing at all. They were always up to something or annoyed about something insignificant.

I walked past the large shamrock on the glass window at Arrivals then international flights. I always took my time because they always ended up chatting to someone, they knew forty years ago. Then, I would be standing there forever waiting for them to come through.

I was certain that when I looked at the ticket it had said the flight was landing at three p.m. and that it had passed. It was three thirty now so they should be getting the suitcases. I watched a mother and son reunite. I watched a mother, and two girls return from a trip wearing matching "I Love Ireland" sweatshirts.

I looked at my watch, it was getting later and later. I saw an Aer Lingus flight attendant at the desk and asked if she could check on the flight.

"I was wondering if you could help me with the party I am waiting for." I asked the young woman behind the desk. She had light brown hair, was slim and had bright green eyes. She was typing what seemed like it had to be The Declaration of Independence. Her name tag read "Fidelma." I had no idea how to pronounce that.

"Hang on just for a second there," She didn't look up.

"Right, no problem." I was getting anxious at this point.

"Now, what can I help you with?" She gave me her full attention this time.

"I wanted to see if my mother and aunt arrived. They were on flight 111 from Shannon." I double checked the little piece of paper I had written down ages ago.

"Yes, I can check right now..." Her voice trailed off. She squinted and then said, "Yes, it has."

"Well, I don't see my mom or my aunt anywhere." My voice was getting shaky. Where were they?

"Tell me their names and I will look at the passenger list." She was waiting to begin typing again.

"Mary Harte and Sr. Margaret Burke." I said fully panicked now.

"No, they weren't on the flight. I could see if they checked in and just missed the flight." She was typing so quickly.

"Yes, that would be great." I said not even really registering what was happening.

"Okay, I have a note here that says they cancelled their tickets this morning." She said it with sympathy and a tone of please don't yell at the messenger.

"What else does it say?" I was furious. They could have called me. They didn't need to drag me all the way out here for no reason. They should have called.

"Nothing, I don't have any other notes." She said quietly.

"Okay, thank you for your help." I said, taking out my cell phone.

I would call Frank and see if he had heard anything.

"Hello, Mary is that you?" Frank obviously had news. He answered on the first ring, so he was taking the information from different people.

"Yes, have you heard anything?" I asked.

"Yes, they cancelled because they are having a special Mass this evening for Aunt Josie. I just got off the phone with your sister, Cathy." I could hear him trying not to laugh.

"You must be joking. They cancelled the flight, didn't tell me and are planning on booking another ticket." I asked.

"Yes, they said their flight gets into Newark Airport at 8 am tomorrow morning." He wasn't laughing that time. He knew he would be taking that trip with me.

The following morning, we had to get up at 6 am to get out to Newark for their arrival. I was exhausted from all the driving the day before. The traffic is also unbearable during that hour.

We parked and headed to arrivals. We only had to wait a few minutes when we saw them coming through the gate. Josie was waving like she was the winner in a Miss America Pageant. Maisie was laughing and holding her white pocketbook.

"Frank, it is so good to see you." Josie leaned right into embrace him. What am I-chopped liver?

"Hi, Mom. What is so funny?" I asked taking the cases.

"Josie got in trouble on the plane. She took a rasher sandwich out of her bag when the stewardess tried to give her the dinner." Mom loved her antics.

"Mary Julia, why can I not enjoy a rasher sandwich I brought with me? I just don't understand why I wasn't supposed to have it." She shook her head.

"You aren't supposed to bring anything that isn't from Duty Free. We went over this." I couldn't believe she still did it.

"Well, I told her it was a sin to throw out food and that she should let me eat it. What harm?" She linked arms with Frank and was ready to go.

"Okay, I am going to get the car. Frank will stay with you, and I will be back." I said, wheeling one of the smaller suitcases to the car.

"That's great. I want to tell Frank all about the beautiful Mass they had in my honor in St. Patrick's in Bullaun. It was beautiful. Wasn't it Maisie?" She already was holding court and we had not even left the airport yet.

I looked back at Mom. She was rolling her eyes. I also happened to notice that she was eating a roll that she obviously pulled out of her purse.

What could I do with them?

Catherine-
The Landmarks

I had a list of all the places that I wanted to see. From the Cliffs of Mohr to Leap Castle, I had many spots I insisted on seeing. Pat took me, no matter where it was in Ireland. I usually dragged my cousins, Caroline, Lorraine, Phil and Patrick. All the landmarks took quite a few trips.

I asked my cousin Patrick, who is Pat's son, to take me to see the house where they filmed Father Ted. We drove around for hours asking everyone where it was. We had to have gone in circles a few times before we found it. My cousin Lorraine and her husband Niall drove around Antrim so we could find the Carrick a Rope Bridge because I saw it on a television show. I asked Caroline to drive me around the Ring of Kerry and made her stop to take photos hanging off the side of the mountain. Phil and I tried to go shopping in Athlone one time, but we didn't make it out of the driveway. We left one of the doors open while reversing and it hit the stone wall. The door bent all the way backwards. It was funny at first, but then.... well, it wasn't. Some of the adventures that I took them on were unforgettable. I still find places to this day.

The journey was about six hours from John F. Kennedy Airport to Shannon Airport in the West of Ireland. It wasn't a bad flight at all. The only reason I found it difficult was because it was a night flight. I wouldn't arrive until six or seven in the morning in Ireland and it was about one or two a.m. in the morning New York time. It was also the jet lag of traveling. However, most of the time my excitement took over.

I loved Ireland so much. My grandmother gave me the gift of experiencing Ireland. Once you visit, you are forever changed. It is not that it is magical or anything, but your whole perspective changes.

Often, I got in line with the same officer because I returned so frequently and at the same time. John, a man in his fifties who liked the full Irish. He was a large man with a round red face and a mess of white hair, but one of the happiest men you could meet. He was always there with a joke or a smile.

"Ah, Catherine-isn't it?" He would smile and put out his hand for my passport.

"Yes, I am back again." I would be happy to see him. He was quite funny.

"Business or......" He would let his voice trail off.

"Pleasure. I will not ever come here for business." I said smiling.

"How many times have you been here?" He would ask.

"One more time than the last time I saw ya." I would be quick enough with the wit.

"One of these days-we must go for a pint. With your cousin Pat, he is here today to collect you, I am sure." He said stamping the passport.

"Yes, except he is a pioneer." I would remind him.

"Oh yes, I forgot that. He could have a mineral and we can have the pint then." He would smile and hand me the passport back.

"Thanks John." I said, going past.

"Good luck and have a brilliant time ya Yank." He laughed, amused, at his own joke.

"Yank-I know you do that to annoy me...." I said laughing.

"We can't all be lucky enough to be Irish." He would say.

"See ya next time, John." I yelled, heading for my suitcase.

I would stand at the luggage carousel for what seemed like a lifetime. This is when jet lag would hit like the flu. Loads of people zoning out or wrestling with their suitcase and nearly falling into the conveyer belt. Babies would be crying, and kids would be whining about hunger or tiredness.

Then I would see my suitcases. I would have one suitcase with my clothes in it, and the other would be for all the presents for everyone. I would have to take all the tags off in case they opened the luggage. I didn't want customs to ever think I was selling Tommy Hilfiger over in Ireland.

After grabbing them, I would walk toward the exit. The automatic doors would open, and I would feel the Irish air hit me in the face. It was beautiful, not something I could describe too well. It made my heart fill up and burst with love and excitement.

In front of me, in the same spot every single time, my cousin Pat was there. We got on as soon as we met. He was fun and quick with the wit. We had met once before in America. He had come over for the St. Patrick's Day Parade in Boston. He would march with firefighters from there. He would wear his full uniform and he couldn't be prouder in the pictures I saw.

Pat would come for me every single time. It didn't matter what time in the morning it was, he was happy to get me. He would ask about the flight and if there was a good-looking guy sitting next to me. The only guy that was ever sitting next to me was a priest. We had a good laugh about that one. He would always start speaking in Irish, then he would translate.

Before one of the trips, I decided I was going to learn enough Irish to be able to say something, even if I couldn't answer him.

We were going through a small town in Clare at that stage. I remember the wall round the bend was painted yellow and black check so motorists could see it. Also, because if it wasn't there when I started speaking Irish Pat may have crashed the car.

"Conas ata tu?" Pat asked. (How are you?)

"Tá mé go maith" I responded. (I am well.)

"Cad is ainm duit?" He asked. (What is your name?)

"Is ainm dom Caitrin." (My name is Catherine)

"Níl agam ach beagáinín Gaeilge."I only speak a little irish.

I could tell it meant so much to him that I had studied and tried to respond to him. He didn't say much for the next few kilometers.

We passed a graveyard and he said to me, "How many people do you think are dead in there?"

"About two hundred or so?" I didn't like being put on the spot and I would get nervous.

"How about all of them?" He would say with a smirk.

I still didn't get it. He had to explain it word for word.

"ALL THE PEOPLE ARE DEAD IN THERE." He would emphasize each word. Then I saw the lightbulb.

"Oh, I get it." We would both laugh at my ways.

We would get back to the house and I would be so excited to see everyone. Kitty, Lorraine, Caroline, Patrick, Phil and Lorraine. The others would come by in the next few days. Annemarie, Brian and John were always around as well.

Pat lit a small light inside me. It was one of faith, family and living in the moment. He also lived for others and made other people safe and taken care of.

Pat traveled to Belarus to help rebuild peoples' lives after Chernobyl. He was a member of the Ballinasloe Sunflowers Association. They organized several fundraising opportunities in Ireland for the people of Belarus.

God called for Pat's help earlier than anyone ever expected. I feel all the emotions all the time. Anger, pain, sadness and most importantly hope. He shared his faith with me that one day I would see him again. Most importantly, he is around me all the time. His energy, love, and goodwill I try to instill in others as well.

Will Shannon ever be the same? No.

Will the journey from the airport ever be the same? No.

But I know he is up there with the rest of my family trying to make our lives better down here. It is a higher power or the values they instilled in me to be a better person. I could be sad that he is not here, but I choose to think of him all the time and I feel peace.

ANNIE-
THE DRESS

It was a gorgeous Saturday. They could be rare enough. We always loved going to the market, but it was usually raining.

I was delighted as it was my 80th birthday party the next day. I had this one dress that I was thinking of wearing, but then Josie said we could have a look in the market in Ballinasloe. They often had lovely dresses that might be perfect for my party

Mary, my niece and the daughter of my brother Tommy (God rest his soul) was coming to collect us. We had all stopped driving ages ago, but that didn't stop us from being out and about. Mary was going to lunch with one of her friends in Hayden's Hotel. She was to drop us off then go to Hayden's and come back around later. Then there was Mass, either in the chapel at Portiuncula Hospital or at St. Michael's Church. Mary usually took us to Church as well because she would be going herself.

Mary collected us at about half eleven. She had on a blue dress with a white trim. She had beautiful dark hair just like her mother Kathleen. She had beautiful blue eyes as well along with a heart of gold. Honestly, you couldn't meet anyone nicer than Mary.

"Isn't it lovely Annie that your sisters were able to come home for your birthday?" Mary was so excited that her aunts were home from New York.

"Ah, yes it….." I was interrupted by Josie.

"We had to come home for it. Even though the flights are twice the price in the summer, it just made sense." Josie always made you feel like she was doing you a favor. She never meant any harm; she was just that way.

As I turned my head, I already saw Maisie beside me rolling her eyes. We were well used to Josie. You couldn't get upset. We would just share a secret laugh or a smile, myself, and Maisie.

When we got to the market in Ballinasloe, Mary parked by the post office, so it was easy enough for all of us. "So, I will be back here for you later, and I will be up in Hayden's for lunch in the meantime. Sure, call into me if you are finished and want to get back to the house or to the Mass. It is up to yourselves." Mary said and she started heading towards Hayden's Hotel.

"Well, I am going to pop to the chemist. I must get some lotion for my hands." Josie said, admiring her own hands. She turned and was off.

"What will we do with her?" I said to Maisie. I linked arms with her, and we headed to look at the dresses.

"I'm delighted for the party tomorrow. I just wish I could find something to wear. I have a beautiful dress and a suit. Mary packed my case and made sure I had choices, but I am not too sure about those ones." She said holding a flowery print dress over her frame.

"That dress is just beautiful. Although, it is a bit like the one you showed me. Maybe you should just leave it." I was about to take it from her and place it on the hanger when I heard Josie shouting from up the road.

"Mind now, hold that dress." She said, pointing at it and quickly moving towards us. She must really love the dress, I thought.

"You mind yourself, Maisie said she wasn't getting it anyway. She said she has something similar." I handed the dress to Josie, and she held it up against her. It really did look beautiful on her, I had to say.

"Isn't it just beautiful? I would be stunning in this. Really classy I think." She said twirling around with it.

"You look wonderful with it." Maisie and I gave each other the eye.

"It is settled then."

The next morning was when we were getting ready for the party. We were all excited about the party. The food and drink would be amazing. I was also looking forward to having the family all together.

"Maisie, do you need help with the zipper of the dress?" I asked because she always had a hard time with that bit.

"This one is not too bad now to be honest." She said from the back room.

I was putting on a bit of makeup when I heard Maisie and Josie shouting. When I reached them, I realized what all the shouting was about.

"Sweet Jesus." It was all I could say.

My two sisters were wearing the same exact dress. Every flower button and seam on it was identical. How could this have happened? One of them would have to change.

"Ah now-you can't both wear the same dress." I said looking at my watch.

"Why can't I? I bought it last year at the fair. So, I had the dress first." Maisie had her hand on her hip.

"Well then it is old looking and I should wear the one I just bought." Josie argued.

"Did ya not notice it was the same dress, Maisie?" I asked wondering how this would end.

"I knew well it was a bit similar-but I didn't pay no mind." Maisie was pleading her case that she should be allowed to wear it.

"Well one of you better change." I said fed up with the nonsense.

Did they listen to me? No, they wore the same dress to me 80th birthday party in spite of the other one. They could be very stubborn.

The worst part was when we got the photos back. We didn't realize the curtains in the restaurant were a remarkably similar pattern to the dresses. You couldn't make it up if ya tried.

CATHERINE- APRIL 25

1010 Wins News would make the sound of a tone to mark the exact time when it hit a certain hour. I had an alarm clock from Radio Shack that was always off by a minute or two. On April 24, 1997, I set the clock according to 1010 Wins News.

My grandmother was in the hospital. She had broken her hip and she was ninety. Everyone tried to avoid having conversations around me. I knew what was going on though. I was painfully aware. I just never wanted it to be the end. I was very lucky to have her for as long as I did. The world was lucky.

The night of the 24th I went to bed. I awoke startled. I knew she was gone. I just knew. I looked at the clock and it was 1:11 am. About a half hour later, the phone rang. It was the hospital calling to tell my mother. I cried all night long. My mother came into my room the next morning and told me that she was gone to heaven. I felt every emotion. It was terrible. I was happy because she wasn't stuck feeling pain in a hospital but devastated that she was gone.

We went through all the motions of organizing the funeral home, the church and the burial. I was writing in my journal, and I remembered that I awoke startled.

I went into my mother's bedroom. She was organizing some papers.

"Mom, what time did Grandma pass away?" I asked slightly above a whisper.

"Last night, I am not sure." she said sadly.

Not wanting to upset her I just left it alone. The wake was filled with so many people from the Church and where my grandmother volunteered. It was so nice to hear about the impact that my grandmother had on others. People that we didn't even know she knew came and told us all about how she touched their lives. It was beautiful.

The funeral was held in her Church. Church of the Visitation. It was where she built her life and made friends that became family. It was where she baptized her children and years later a funeral for her husband.

I stood in front of the church and spoke of how wonderful she was as a mother, a sister, wife, aunt, friend, cousin and my grandmother. I knew the harder days were to come.

I didn't know how to live now. I would pick up the phone to call her only to realize she was no longer here.

Of course, she was old, and it was to be expected. It didn't make me feel any better though. Everyone would just say the same thing over and over again.

It wasn't until I was much older that I realized what I had to do. I had to tell her story.

Maisie never worried about what other people thought of her. It is extremely difficult to accomplish something like that. She was just herself and comfortable in herself. Even if someone was wrong to her or gave her a tough time, she would just roll her eyes and move on. She didn't carry a grudge or hold onto to anything negative.

"There are loads of people in this world Cathy. They aren't all going to like you. Keep going until you find the ones that do. Be happy today. That is all there really is to it all." She would tell me things like that all the time in all different ways.

April 25th was always the worst day of the year for me. It was the anniversary of her death. I knew she didn't want me to be sad. I just couldn't help it. No matter what, I braced for the worst feelings every time it came along.

It wasn't until many years later that everything changed. Maisie had sent me an enormously powerful sign. The signs are everywhere. It is just a matter of your faith and if you truly believe.

I met him. I had known him for a long time, but not in a personal way. Suddenly I was drawn to him. We began spending time together and it was wonderful. We decided that we were going to go out to dinner and see how that went.

As I was getting ready, I glanced over at the calendar. It was a Saturday, so I wasn't thinking about the actual date. It was Saturday, April 25, 2015. I realized that he could be the one. It had to be her that had set this up.

I didn't want to get caught up in it. I may have been trying to make it work then. I remember thinking, "Whatever happens is meant to be. I am going to go and try to have a nice time."

We were married a year and a half later. We chose October 1, 2016, as a wedding date.

I also discovered in my research that she landed on American soil on October 1, 1928.

Like I said before, the signs are all there. Are you looking for the signs?

CATHERINE-
I WAITED TOO LONG

I waited too long. I thought my mother would live until I was old. I thought Nolan would have his grandmother, my mother, for as long as I had Maisie. Turns out he had about three years with his Mumsey.

She is physically here. She stays in her room most days and does not really want to do anything except stare blankly at the television. She knows who I am but does not understand many things. She struggles with names and relationships. I remind her how she knows people quite often.

"Your mom has frontotemporal dementia. I believe she has had it for some time." I knew the doctor was going to say something about dementia. But it does not stop you from hoping that she will say something else. *My mother* wasn't going to have dementia. She was only seventy and you were not supposed to get that until you were in your mid-eighties. Apparently not.

"What now?" I asked, thinking there would be medication or a doctor that could help. It turns out this is a question that I ask myself every day.

"There is a memory patch. It might help." I wasn't processing what she was saying. We were on a Zoom virtual appointment. She said *might*.

Most people would run around and get second opinions. I knew it was true. We had a full workup-neurology, cardiac, endocrinology, psychological evaluation along with MRI's and a spinal tap.

When I think back, it really started many years ago. Having to repeat conversations or forgetting events was the most recurring issue. She stopped driving because it was difficult to see at night. Then, she stopped driving in the day because she felt her perception was off.

I decided to take her to the eye doctor. I thought she was losing her vision. I flipped the magazine in the waiting room while she was in with the doctor. One of the staff members came out.

"The doctor needs to see you." She had a concerned look on her face.

"Coming." I put the magazine back in the rack with the others. I had no idea what she was going to tell me.

"Good afternoon. You are Mary's daughter? Nice to meet you." He put out his hand. My mom sat on the examining table, and he stood by a projection of her eye on the wall.

"Yes, nice to meet you as well." I responded.

"Well, your mother needs to be seen by her primary doctor. I see evidence of a stroke in her eye. If you look here how it is" he said pointed to a chart in the dark. I had no idea what I was looking at. The look in his face told me it was serious.

I made an appointment with a neurologist, psychologist, neurological psychologist, and a geriatric doctor. It was just testing and forwarding tests from one doctor to another. There were medical release forms, and my mother couldn't hold a pen in her hand.

It wasn't until the doctor asked her to count backwards from one hundred. My mother looked at me as if she asked her to do something she had never heard of. Then she asked her who the President of the United States is. At the time it was Trump. My mother looked around the room and then at the floor. "Bush. Yes, the son." She said proudly.

I felt like I was going to scream and burst into tears at the time. Why was she getting the questions wrong? I was talking to her all the time. She didn't seem like she didn't know what was going on. The doctor asked her to draw a square on a piece of paper and a clock. She made a list of excuses about having nothing to lean on, glasses missing and after getting angry the doctor told her not to worry about it.

A clock. A square. My mother, an emergency room nurse for twenty-five years- could not draw a clock. The woman who tells me that she knew everything I would just by looking at my face. It was true, she always knew when I was up to something. She was the woman who could plan a funeral for someone who suddenly died. She was a PTA mom who made cupcakes from scratch at eight o'clock at night the night before a last-minute party. She was a woman who lost her father at twelve years old and grew up so fast. She wasn't supposed to get dementia.

It is my soul that is in agony. I never know what to think or what to say. At first, I tried to make everything better. I was going to take care of her. I would bring her to my house, have all the holidays and just make everything fine.

"Mom, do you want to come live with me?" I asked her after one of the doctor's appointments.

"No, I want to live in my own house. Well, one of them." She said.

"Oh, where is the other house?" I asked.

"In the Bronx. Oh, you think I am crazy, don't you?" She looked angry in her eyes suddenly.

"No, I just wasn't sure which one you were talking about." I had to get on board.

"Yes, the one on 238th Street. Cathy, have you seen my mother? It would just be easier if I could just talk to her. She would make sense of all this and explain it to you." She got up and started taking things out of her drawers and putting them in other drawers. I noticed that she had not had her hair done in quite some time.

"No, I didn't see her today." Fortunately, I had read some information on dementia. When they look for someone that has passed, they have forgotten. If I tell her that she has passed away, it may be like the first time she has heard that. My grandmother was passed by almost twenty-five years at this point. I took a deep breath and tried to hold in tears.

"Oh, okay." She said going through the drawers like nothing unusual had happened.

I didn't see it as a dangerous situation until a few months later. My mother called me in the evening one night.

"Cathy, can you order more thyroid pills for me?" She asked.

"Sure, you have two different pills. Which one?" I asked pulling up the prescriptions on the computer.

"Oh, I only have one now. I just need that one filled." She said as I heard her emptying pills into a container.

"Let me come see, I will be there in a bit." I said hanging up the phone.

On the drive down was when I began to get nervous. She knew her pills and the dosages. What was this about?

When I arrived, she had her pill box container on the bed. It was a hat box that she made into a medicine cabinet. She pointed to it.

I opened the hat box and drew a breath from the deepest part of my soul. There were dozens of pills scattered at the bottom of the hat box. The tops were off and there was a large aspirin container she was holding onto tightly.

"I just get them from here." She said shaking the bottle.

"Mom, YOU CAN'T DO THIS." I immediately regretted yelling.

"Look, I am sorry for yelling. I really am. Let us look at this together. Can you show me how you do your pills for the week?" I was trying to assess the situation as best as I could.

She took the aspirin bottle that was filled with many unusual types of pills- mostly her prescriptions- and shook out a handful. She began randomly placing them on different days.

I reminded myself of what my face must have looked like. Deep breath so I don't create a sense of panic.

"Mom, why don't you let me take the pills home and organize them for you?" I said calmly.

She hesitated and then took a breath.

"Ok, I guess." She said defeated.

"Mom, they are small to see the writing on them. I have to get a magnifying glass to see that." I said packing up the pills.

"Yes, they are really small. I am sure that is what happened, why I have them mixed up." She said relieved.

"So, I will go through them and then organize them for you." I spoke. I had to hold back the tears and the pain in my chest and stomach. I didn't want her to realize the magnitude of what was happening.

How could a woman who could tell I was up to no good not be able to complete a simple task? I didn't understand it and I was in denial.

Don't wait, it will be too late. To tell them you love them, to show them you care, to listen to their story from fifty years ago (even though you heard it a million times).

You will drive by their house wishing they were still there when it is too late.

You will want to hear the story just one more time.

You will always feel sadness. It is part of life. What you don't want to feel is regret.